HEART

OF THE

Devil

FORGE TRILOGY BOOK THREE

THIS IS NO LONGER THE PROPERTY
OF THE SEATTLE PUBLIC LIBRARY

MEGHAN

NEW YORK TIMES BESTSELLING AUTHOR

MARCH

Received On:

APR 1 ᵕ 2019

Fremont Library

CONTENTS

Heart of the Devil v
About This Book vii

1. Forge 1
2. India 7
3. Forge 14
4. India 18
5. Forge 28
6. India 31
7. India 38
8. India 46
9. Forge 58
10. India 65
11. Forge 69
12. India 71
13. Forge 78
14. India 81
15. India 86
16. Forge 91
17. India 96
18. India 106
19. Forge 109
20. India 111
21. Forge 114
22. India 118
23. Forge 124
24. India 126
25. India 132
26. Forge 138
27. India 142

28. India   148
29. India   151
30. India   160
31. India   165
32. Forge   171
33. India   173
34. Forge   181
35. India   184
36. Forge   187
37. India   192
38. Forge   194
39. India   196
40. Forge   199
41. India   204
42. India   207
43. Forge   211
44. India   216
45. Forge   219
46. India   225
47. Forge   229
48. Forge   237
    Epilogue   242

    Acknowledgments   249
    Also by Meghan March   251
    About the Author   255

HEART OF THE DEVIL

Book Three of the Forge Trilogy

Meghan March

Copyright © 2018 by Meghan March LLC

All rights reserved.

Editor: Pam Berehulke, Bulletproof Editing,

www.bulletproofediting.com

Cover Design: Letitia Hassar, R.B.A. Designs,

www.rbadesigns.com

Cover photo:

No part of this book may be reproduced or transmitted in any form or by any means, electronic or mechanical, including photocopying, recording, or by any information storage and retrieval system without the written permission of the author, except for the use of brief quotations in a review.

This book is a work of fiction. Names, characters, places, and incidents are either products of the author's imagination or are used fictitiously. Any resemblance to actual persons, living or dead, events, or locales is entirely coincidental. The author acknowledges the trademarked status and trademark owners of various products referenced in this work of fiction, which have been used without permission. The publication/use of these trademarks is not authorized, associated with, or sponsored by the trademark owners.

Visit my website at www.meghanmarch.com.

It started as a game. She was nothing but my pawn.

But I was quick to see the error in my ways, and now she is everything I never knew I needed.

The value of a woman like India Baptiste is beyond measure.

But the problem with being a man like me? I've already screwed this up, and there's no guarantee India will take me on for one last bet.

I'll do what ever I have to do. Drop to my knows and offer her the only thing I have left. The one thing that's only ever been hers—the heart of the devil.

Heart of the Devil is the third book in the Forge Trilogy and should be read after *Deal with the Devil* and *Luck of the Devil.*

FORGE

Ten years ago

"What the fuck was that?"

The floor-to-ceiling panes of glass in my office just rattled so hard, I thought they would shatter. I jumped out of my seat at the desk and rushed to the windows in time to see a ball of fire explode on the water halfway between Isaac's island and Ibiza.

Fire on the water. Every captain's worst nightmare, and this one was growing by the minute.

Through the thick cloud of black smoke, I could make out a sleek red hull. The other boat involved in the crash was indistinguishable, hidden behind the expanding wall of flame.

Fuck.

Bolting from my office, I snagged the keys lying on the counter in Isaac's spacious kitchen and ran out of the house, heading for the stairs carved into the cliff that led down to the dock.

I'd lost track of time as I'd worked, and I had no idea how long Isaac had been gone. He took his small fishing boat out to catch lunch for his birthday, because according to him, there was no day better spent. I'd been planning to go with him, but a call had come in that couldn't be ignored.

Pirates off the coast of Africa had been spotted stalking one of Isaac's ships. Isaac had winked and told me to handle it.

"You're more than capable. That's why you'll inherit the fleet and everything I've built someday. God put you on my ship for a reason. You're my legacy, Jericho."

The memory faded away as I pounded down the dock to the tender bobbing on the waves. It wasn't fancy, since we mostly used it to fetch supplies from Ibiza, but it would get me to the wreck quickly so I could offer assistance to the survivors of whatever the fuck happened out there.

I started the engine, tossed off the lines, and hammered the throttle, expecting to see a swarm of boats heading toward the accident to help, but there was only one nearby. As I cut through the water, closing the distance at top speed, I caught sight of one boat involved in the collision as the bow shot above the surface as if taking its last breath, then sank quickly.

"No!" An icy fist seized my heart as the sea claimed the familiar black outline of a woman's profile set against the white of the hull.

Donatella's profile.

The love of Isaac's life. The woman who died in an accident, while he was at sea and totally unaware. He never forgave himself for not being there, and as long as I'd known him, he'd put her image on every single ship he owned.

I scanned the water, desperately searching for Isaac's silver hair, expecting his sure strokes to be carrying him away from the fire and toward the nearest boat, but I didn't see him.

A man on the rescue vessel hauled a kid over the side. *Thank fuck for that.* I piloted around the blaze, trying to find Isaac, but another explosion sent flames spiraling from the surface as the boat with the red hull exploded.

Shit!

"Isaac!" I screamed his name, praying like hell he was swimming toward the other boat. I turned toward them and called out to see if they'd rescued him, but the captain didn't answer as he pulled someone else from the water. I froze, but the momentary hope shattered when I saw a younger man climb onto the swim platform.

I yelled again, and the last man out of the water spotted me. Instead of replying, he snarled at the captain, shoving him toward the helm.

"Go! Go! Go! Get us the fuck out of here!"

What the hell?

I didn't recognize him, but when the captain stared at him instead of moving, the blond man charged toward the helm, pushing the kid and the two other men aside as he grabbed the wheel. In moments, the boat roared away from the fire, leaving any remaining survivors behind.

Who the fuck does that? I wasn't fucking leaving until I was certain every single survivor had been rescued.

"Isaac!" I bellowed until my voice turned ragged, circling the debris field, desperate to find him. On my second pass, I spotted a hand clinging to a floating cooler.

Thank God. I pulled the throttle back into neutral and charged to the side of the boat.

"I'm coming, Isaac. I'm coming." *I swear to Christ, I'll save you.*

With that vow, I launched myself over the side, diving below the burning surface of the water before emerging inside the ring of fire. To my right, a hand rose above the water, and I swam toward it.

"Isaac!" I reached out, sending up a prayer as soon as I saw his dive watch, but when my fingers touched the skin, I knew something was wrong. I tugged, and the arm flew toward me . . . but there was no body connected.

No. No!

Gas- and oil-laced water rushed into my mouth as I screamed his name again and again. Ice-cold rage flooded my veins as I realized what had likely happened. *Those motherfuckers fled the scene of a crime. They* hit *Isaac's boat and fucking ran.*

But that didn't matter right now. All that mattered was finding Isaac. *The rest of Isaac.*

"Isaac!"

But there was no reply, except the crackle of the fire and the scent of burning oil, gas, plastic . . . and human flesh.

I sank beneath the surface, not caring that the sea water stung as I opened my eyes, searching the submerged wreckage for any sign of the only father I'd ever known.

The hull of the red boat faded as it sank to its grave on the bottom of the ocean, joining Isaac's.

Isaac has to be down there. He must have been close to the impact or the initial explosion.

I kicked to the surface, my hand still gripping Isaac's as I swam for my boat to climb aboard to get my mask. Moments later, I was back in the water, having left the only piece of Isaac I might find, and dove to the bottom.

I wouldn't rest until I found the rest of him . . . and the fucking coward who left him here to die.

2

INDIA

Present day

Terror and fear race through my body unchecked as I stare at the man who just stepped out of the elevator into the lobby of the penthouse floor and my own personal nightmare.

My husband is missing, and Donnigan, Bates, and Goliath are dead.

Belevich's gaze sweeps over my bloodstained dress, and his eyes go wide.

"Did you kill them? *Where is he?*" My shrill questions come out ragged and desperate, and the Russian stares at me like I've lost my goddamned mind.

"Kill who?" Belevich asks. He takes a careful step toward me, like he's afraid I'm going to snap. And I might.

"Don't you dare come any fucking closer to me. Answer my goddamned questions." If Belevich had anything to do with this, I'm not going to make killing me easy for him. I'll punch, kick, and claw his goddamned eyes out.

"I was playing poker, India. At the same goddamned table as you. I didn't kill anyone."

"Then who the fuck did this? Where is my husband?" My voice rises to ear-piercing levels as I point down the hall.

"I don't know anything, but—" Belevich's head swivels to follow the direction of my shaking arm, and he finally sees Bates lying with his neck at an awkward angle, and Donnigan's body with the blood-stained carpet beneath him. "Jesus Christ. What the fuck happened?"

"I don't fucking know!"

Belevich crouches, checking Bates and Donnigan's necks for pulses he won't find. I know, because I checked them both too.

They're dead. They're all dead. A sob threatens to break free from my lips, but I swallow it as Belevich draws a gun from an ankle holster and jumps to his feet.

"You fucking liar!" I scream, fisting my hands as I shrink toward the corner. Belevich isn't taking me out without a fight.

"I'm not going to kill you, Indy. I don't know what the fuck happened here, but you need to get behind me."

I blink at him as he waves to where he expects me to stand. *What? No. I'm not going near him.*

A man groans from the hallway I ran down only minutes before after frantically searching for Jericho in our room. I dart toward Belevich so I can get a better view.

Please, God, let it be Jericho. Tell me I missed him somehow.

Belevich tries to block me with his body, but I sidestep him so I can see. The sliver of hope I'm clutching disintegrates. Jericho isn't walking toward us. It's Goliath, and blood gushes from his chest with each stumbling step he takes down the carpeted hallway.

Belevich cocks the gun. "Is he yours, or does he die?"

"He's with me. Don't shoot him!" I shove past Belevich, skirt around Bates and Donnigan's bodies, and run toward Goliath, who I thought was dead only moments ago. From the amount of blood he's losing, he still might die soon. "Stop. Sit down. We need to get you help."

Goliath's knees buckle, and I drop to a crouch beside him.

"We need towels. Sheets. Something to stop the bleeding."

"I will get them." Belevich steps around me to stride down the hall and kick open a door to a housekeeping closet. Moments later, he drops a stack of towels onto the carpet next to me.

"Move aside," he orders, and I stumble back on my heels as he pulls Goliath's hand away from where blood gushes. His shoulder, not his chest. Belevich dabs at it with the towel, peering close to get a better look before using Goliath's hand to hold it against the wound.

"Is he—" I start to ask, but Belevich interrupts.

"Keep pressure on it," he tells Goliath. "Your lucky day that you bled enough for them to think you were dead."

"Did you see who did this? Who took Jericho?" I ask as I clench a towel in my hands. "We have to find him."

Belevich hands Goliath another towel to replace the one that is already soaked through with blood. "Give the man a second to stop bleeding before you question him."

I whip my head sideways to stare daggers at Belevich. "We don't have time. He could already be dead."

Goliath opens his mouth to speak, but all that comes out is a groan and a curse. "Fuck . . ."

Belevich tears the final towel into strips and winds them around Goliath's shoulder to secure the makeshift bandage.

"Questions can wait until we get out of here. If we are discovered with the bodies, the police will hold us all for questioning for days. And you're right—with every minute that passes, the chance of finding your husband alive disappears."

My stomach roils, and bile climbs in my throat. "Leave . . . leave Bates and Donnigan? But—"

"Do you want to see your husband again?"

The ice water that seems to have replaced my blood freezes. "Yes, of course I want to see my husband again."

"Good. Then we go." He rises and offers a hand to Goliath. The large man stands on unsteady legs, but we each reach out to support him.

"Service elevator is at the other end of the hall from this one," Belevich says.

I shoot a suspicious stare at him. "How do you know? Why are you even helping us?"

Goliath grunts as we take the first step down the hall, and blood is already seeping through the makeshift bandage.

Fuck, he needs a doctor.

Belevich keeps walking, steadying Goliath with one hand as he grips the pistol in the other. "Because you're the daughter of one of the most influential men in Russia. A man whose favor I would like to be in."

My father.

Another wave of chills ripples across my skin. *I didn't even think of him.*

"Could he . . . could he have done this?"

Goliath replies to my question with a shake of his

head that makes him groan. "They were young. Wearing balaclavas."

"This is not Federov's style," Belevich says, agreeing. He pauses in front of the door smeared with blood, probably from Goliath's hands as he stumbled out. *The entrance to the penthouse suite that Jericho and I shared.* "If you want any of your shit, run and get it now so we can get the fuck out of here before we all get arrested."

The clothes inside mean nothing to me. Nothing means anything to me except Jericho.

Fuck. Fuck. Tears burn the back of my eyes as another wave of despair washes over me. *This can't be happening. This can't be real.* But it is, and I don't have time to cry.

I gather every bit of fortitude I have and blink back the tears. "I don't need anything except my husband. Let's go."

"Good. Then we go," Belevich replies.

When we reach the service elevator, I punch the call button. As we wait, my thoughts race.

"Are you sure it couldn't be Federov? Wouldn't he have motive?"

Belevich's blond hair swishes across his collar as he shakes his head. "What motive could he have? From what I have heard, all he wants is to be reunited with his daughter. Not buy her animosity for life by kidnapping her husband."

I pray he's right, because Jericho's life depends on it.

"Then can he help us find him?" I ask, not sure if it's a viable solution, but right now, I need all the big guns we can find.

"Perhaps," Belevich says. "He may be able to help."

"What about Koba?" My shoulders stiffen as I look up at Goliath. "Where the hell is Koba? What happened to him?"

Goliath's brows dip together and his nostrils flare. "Fucking traitor. I knew it." His black eyes focus on me. "We find him, and we'll find Forge."

Scenes flash through my brain—

Koba unable to get to me when the man sliced my side and snatched my purse in Saint-Tropez.

Koba still in his car when Alanna's efficiency unit was being trashed . . . and not able to catch up with the kid who took off running.

"I'm going to kill him myself if anyone so much as harms one hair on Jericho's head." I look from Belevich to Goliath. "Let's go. I want my husband back."

3

FORGE

*T*he memory of the day I pulled Isaac's body from the wreckage of his boat batters my brain until I finally open my eyes.

Instead of light, I'm surrounded by darkness. As I change position, fabric rubs against my face, so I reach up to push it away but can't move my arms. My wrists are bound behind my back, and when I yank against the binding to free myself, thin pieces of plastic cut into my skin. *Zip ties.* My ankles are trussed too.

What the fuck?

I open my mouth to speak, but my lips are sealed shut. *Duct tape.*

I lie still on my side as I try to figure out what the hell happened. My brain feels like I'm swimming through the ocean in the dead of night, in a fog. Something's not right. *Was I drugged?* I try to piece together how the fuck I ended up here.

Indy's poker game. Prague.

Fuck. *Indy. Please fucking tell me they didn't get her too.*

My memory is fuzzy, but I remember being on the phone in the hotel room before the door crashed open and masked men rushed inside. Gunshots popping through suppressers. Goliath yelling. Spinning around to see Donnigan going down before he could get a shot off. They rushed me, and I swear I got in a few punches before everything went black, but I don't remember.

Jesus fucking Christ. Who the fuck did this?

I stretch out my arms and legs, feeling around and trying to get any sense of where I am. I'm praying Indy isn't tied up in here with me. *Please fucking tell me she's safe at the hotel.*

My face is pressed against a floor that vibrates against my jaw, and my fingers brush a rubber mat. I breathe in the acrid scent of exhaust. I'm in a vehicle. Maybe a van? Or the back of a truck?

My foot hits something. I try to say Indy's name, but it comes out as a garbled series of grunts.

If they took her . . . I will burn down the entire fucking world if that's what it takes to free us both.

Nothing touches her. No one hurts her. Ever.

But I did. I took her. Used her. Kidnapped her.

The recriminations rip through me. *I never should have pushed her to bet that fucking room key. I never should have gone after her in Monte Carlo.*

Regrets seize me as the tip of my shoe catches on a pant leg.

It's not Indy. She was wearing a dress. So, who . . . ?

A boot connects with my back, and lightning bolts of pain shoot down my spine.

"Do not move," a man barks out with a Russian accent.

Russian. Fuck.

That means either Federov lost his patience with me about meeting Indy and decided to get me out of the way once and for all, or Belevich has ulterior motives that I somehow missed.

He was at the game at La Reina . . . and Mallorca. Why didn't I investigate him?

Because I was caught up with Indy. And now she's in danger because of me.

I have to get away. Have to get to her.

As the pain dissipates from the boot to my back, I try to picture the inside of what I assume is a cargo van and guess where the man who spoke could be sitting. I swing my body around to kick out at him. As soon as my feet slam into bone, he barks something out in Russian before someone grabs my feet and ties them down.

As something sharp stabs into my neck and darkness rushes in, one thought repeats in my brain.

Must. Save. Indy.

*B*elevich texts someone from inside the elevator, but the Cyrillic alphabet on his phone screen might as well be Greek to me. With his good hand, Goliath slides his cell from his pocket, and the screen is covered with green bubbles indicating notifications.

"Jericho?" I ask, desperation turning my words ragged.

"Not yet," he replies with a pained grunt.

My apprehension climbs with each passing minute, and I hope like hell that I'm making the right choice by going with him. Goliath stays glued to my side as we exit the service elevator into a parking garage. A black G-Wagen pulls up to the loading zone, and Goliath and I tense.

"Come. Come. It's my driver." Belevich takes a step

forward, but Goliath doesn't move as he looks down at me.

"Do we go?" I whisper.

Goliath's jaw clenches, and the lines around his eyes deepen. He has to be racked with pain. I don't know what else to do.

Instead of replying, Goliath nods. "Okay."

"Come. Hurry," Belevich says, leading us toward the boxy Mercedes SUV. The driver jumps out to open the door to the back seat and helps Goliath inside. Belevich takes the front passenger seat, and I slide in beside Goliath.

I'm questioning every decision I'm making, but I don't know what else to do. I don't know who I can trust, and my gut twists at the thought of how we left Donnigan and Bates behind. *I'm so sorry.* I send up the apology and promise silently that I'll make it right as soon as Goliath, who slumps against the door when the SUV begins moving, isn't bleeding out, and we find Jericho.

Belevich rattles off orders in Russian, and I've never wished I spoke a language more.

Goliath groans as we roll over a speed bump at the entrance to the parking garage.

"Where are we going? Goliath needs help," I tell Belevich.

He twists in his seat to look back at us both, his stare fixing on the blood-soaked towel around Goliath's shoulder. "I have a friend not far from here. She can help him."

"Is she a doctor?"

"A veterinarian," Belevich replies.

"A vet? Really?"

"Better than nothing, and she won't report a gunshot wound to the authorities, who will drag us all in for interrogation and fleeing the scene of a crime."

A chunk of ice settles in my stomach, and I remind myself that beggars can't be choosers. Right now, I'll do whatever I have to do to find Jericho and make sure Goliath doesn't die.

"Okay. What then? What do we do? How are we going to find him?" There's no question who the *him* I'm referring to is.

"I will call in a few favors . . ."

As he trails off, I lean forward in the seat, gripping the door as we careen out of the parking garage. Sirens wail in the street toward the hotel entrance.

Fuck. Fuck. Fuck.

"We made it out just in time," Belevich says as our vehicle hugs the curb to let the police through. We all watch the flashing lights as they pass us.

"They're going to be looking for me and Jericho," I whisper, thankful they can't see us through the blacked-out windows of the SUV.

"Of course," Belevich says. "But they move too slow. If we rely on them, you will never find Forge."

Due to my unusual childhood, I've never been one to trust law enforcement, so I'm inclined to agree with him. "Tell me about these favors. How fast can you call them in, and how can they help us? What do you need from me?"

Belevich glances over his shoulder into the back seat. "You really do want to find him, don't you?"

I blink twice, repeating his question in my brain. "Of course I want to find him. He's my husband."

"But the reasons he married you . . . they didn't have anything to do with the reason a man normally marries a woman, from what I heard."

I'm reminded then that Belevich knows too much about things he shouldn't. Like that my sister was kidnapped and was going to be sold as a sex slave if I didn't pay the ransom to get her back.

"What's your angle, Belevich? Who the fuck are you, really?" I ask, wishing we'd had this conversation before I got into a vehicle with him and my very injured bodyguard, who won't be much help if we're truly in danger.

"Right now, I'm one of the only friends you have in this country. Like I said, I want to be in your father's favor. That's my angle."

I shrink closer to Goliath's side of the car. As if he can sense my unease, Goliath reaches out a hand to cover mine, giving it a quick squeeze against the cool black leather.

"Good luck with that, since I don't even know the man, but suit yourself."

The Mercedes takes a series of quick turns down the narrow streets, and five minutes later, we park in front of a building that has seen better days. What looks like fresh graffiti marks a side door that is flanked by two barred windows.

If it didn't say VETERINÁŘ above the doorway in faded red letters on a white sign, I would have thought I'd made a horrible error in judgment. I may not speak Czech, but even I can translate that.

"Come. We will go through the side door. It leads to the treatment rooms. The dogs will not tell on us." Belevich pushes open his door of the SUV and climbs out.

I turn toward Goliath, letting my indecision and fear show on my face. "Our only other choice is to run. What do you think we should do?"

Belevich's driver sits ahead of me, listening to every word, but I don't care. I need to get Goliath's read on the situation, because right now, I don't know if my decisions are leading us astray.

"Let's go inside," Goliath says as he discreetly lifts the side of his suit jacket to show me a flash of metal.

He has a gun. Thank God. Why didn't he pull it on Belevich before? *Oh, wait, that's right, he was bleeding out from his shoulder.*

"Okay. Then we'll go," I say as Belevich opens Goliath's door.

"Come on. Come on. We don't want to be seen, even if the people in this neighborhood do not like the police any more than we do."

I slide across the leather seat, and it only takes a few steps to cross the cracked sidewalk and slip through the open door.

Inside, fluorescent lighting turns the dingy white floor a sickly yellow. Disinfectant mixed with wet-dog scent assails my nostrils as we step inside. Meows and barks and whines come from several directions, and my instincts charge into overdrive as I follow Goliath and Belevich into a room with a stainless-steel table in the center.

"Really, Dmitri?" a feminine voice says. "I don't hear from you for over a year, and now twice in two days? And you bring me a bleeding man? You are good in bed, but not that good."

I peer around Goliath's massive form as a fair-skinned woman in blue scrubs props her hands on her hips and glares at Belevich.

"Marina, please. You are saving this man's life. And perhaps the life of another. You will be rewarded hand-somely, I promise." Belevich presses a kiss to her cheek just below a lock of dark hair escaping from her surgical cap.

"I do not want your money. You know this."

Belevich takes her latex-glove-covered hand in his. "You will have my eternal gratitude, and I promise I will show you next time that I *am* that good in bed."

Clearly, these two have a close relationship, because Marina yanks her hand from Belevich's, rolls her eyes, and motions for Goliath to sit down on the metal table.

"Now I must scrub in again before I can touch him. Hands off until we are done, Mitri."

Marina is all business as she hustles over to the sink and rips off her gloves. She scours her skin roughly with soap and steaming hot water.

I say nothing as I find a place against the wall that allows me to see the door and everyone in the room. *Ah, situational awareness, my old friend.*

When she has donned new gloves, Marina marches over to Goliath. "What happened to you?"

"Didn't move quick enough." Goliath's voice is strained from the pain.

She reaches for the towel, but pauses, and looks at me and then Belevich. "Both of you, out. Send my assistant. She will know what to do. There are chairs in the break room. Stay out of sight."

I swallow and meet Goliath's black gaze.

He inclines his chin. "I'll be fine, Mrs. Forge."

Just hearing him call me by my married name sends a stab of urgency through me. *I have to find Jericho.*

"Okay. I won't be far," I tell him before following Belevich out of the room.

In the hallway, he waves over a younger woman in

rainbow scrubs. "Your boss needs you. Is there anyone else here?"

She shakes her head at the Russian. "No. We are closed. Dr. Novotny and I were only staying late to look after one of the dogs who had surgery this afternoon."

"Good. Go help Marina."

As soon as the girl disappears into the treatment room and closes the door behind her, Belevich eyes me.

"You look like hell."

I glance down at the dress I'm wearing, now stained with even more blood. "I don't care what I look like. We need to start calling in your favors."

He jerks his head toward the door that just closed. "That's favor number one. Before I call in another, I need to know who the hell has balls big enough to kidnap Jericho Forge. You tell me, and then we can get started."

One name comes to my mind instantly. *Bastien de Vere.*

But would he . . . ?

"De Vere," Belevich says before I can answer my own silent question.

"But he wasn't here. How could he have done it?"

Belevich takes a few steps down the hallway and pushes open another door. He waves me over as he enters. I peek inside to see the employee break room Marina mentioned. Inside a small card table, two chairs, a mini fridge, a microwave, and a coffee maker.

Belevich helps himself to a bottle of water from the fridge and tosses me one too. "It's not vodka, but it will do for right now."

He pulls out both chairs and motions for me to take the one opposite him as he sits.

"Do you not think it is strange that de Vere did not come? He has made a habit of following you everywhere he can, has he not? Like Mallorca. He did not play, but he came to watch you. Make trouble for you."

My mind instantly dredges up the memory of what Jericho said about the chopper being tampered with, preventing my security detail and me from taking it home.

"That night . . . in Mallorca, I thought he was up to something. It was like he didn't want me to be able to leave."

"De Vere has always wanted you. No one can miss that. But he cannot have you as long as your husband is in the way."

"But—" I start to say something, then snap my lips shut.

"What?" Belevich asks after he takes a swig of his water.

My mind goes to that evening in Alanna's apartment, and how Bastien's employee's little brother had stashed a suitcase there with my stuff and enough drugs to get me sentenced to years in prison.

"He doesn't want me anymore," I say as I twist open the cap of the water.

"Why would you say that?"

I take a sip and decide I have nothing to lose by telling Belevich what happened. When I finish, he leans on the two back legs of the chair and motions at me with his now empty bottle.

"That is interesting, but it does not mean what you think. If de Vere cannot have you, maybe he does not want anyone to have you. Then again, if he got rid of Forge, he would change his tune quickly. After all, you are the daughter of one of the world's richest men. Even de Vere couldn't walk away from a temptation like that. Especially now that he's been cut off by his family."

I swallow a lump that rose in my throat as he spoke. "Are you sure . . . totally sure . . . that my father wouldn't . . ." I try to figure out how to phrase the question I want to ask, but Belevich doesn't need to hear it.

"Federov would not kidnap Forge. From what I know, the two men have much respect for each other." Belevich leans forward, and the legs of the chair hit the floor. "Which is why you are right—we should call your father for help."

I jerk awake as someone grips my hands and another person grabs my feet.

Through my duct-tape gag, I yell, but I'm trussed up like a fucking swine that's about to be spit roasted as they haul me out of the van. Hinges squeak and footsteps echo on concrete as I breathe in the scent of blood.

Another door groans as it opens, sending cold air over my face, and goose bumps rise on my skin. The temperature must have dropped twenty degrees, but we're not outside anymore.

My hands are lifted above my head and hooked over something. *Fuck.* It's a walk-in cooler. As soon as my feet are released, my entire body weight jerks at my shoulders as gravity kicks in. I dangle, unable to touch my bound feet to the floor.

"Boss?" a man asks.

"Coming," another man with a Russian accent replies.

Someone steps close enough for me to feel his body heat, but I can't see anything with my eyes covered until someone shoves the fabric up. I blink in the dim light, trying to focus on the pale blue eyes staring back at me. The rest of his face is obscured by a balaclava. He reaches out and tears away the duct tape covering my mouth with one quick yank, taking skin off with it.

I swipe my tongue out to taste blood once more and grit my teeth together. Focusing on how badly I want to rip his head from his body, I push everything else aside.

"I don't know who the fuck you are or who's paying you, but—"

His mouth opens and he huffs out a laugh. "Let me guess. You can pay me more to double-cross them? Original." His accent is solidly eastern European, and my gut clenches.

He can't be working for Federov. Federov wouldn't fucking do this. Would he? That's the billion-dollar question. I pissed him off, and I've heard plenty of stories about his ruthless reprisals before, but I never thought he'd dare with me.

"Take the fucking mask off, you piece of shit. Let me see your face. Tell me who you work for." I bark out the orders, knowing that they won't be followed, but I still have to try.

"Who I work for will not matter, because you will

die, Forge . . . and then what will happen to that pretty little wife of yours?"

As soon as he mentions Indy, rage turns to ice in my veins. *They can torture me. Peel the fucking skin from my body. But if they fucking dare touch one hair on her head . . . I'll burn the entire world down.*

"You motherfuck—" I swing backward, using the momentum to lift my legs and kick out at him, but a blow from behind cracks against the back of my skull, and my entire body goes limp as blackness invades once more.

6

INDIA

I stare at Belevich like he's sprouted a second head. "You really think my father would help?"

Having never had a father, I've never had one to ask for help, so it's a completely foreign concept to me. *Why would a man I don't know help me?*

"Yes. Of course he would. And even though we are not in Russia, his power extends beyond borders."

Under normal circumstances, I might be intimidated by the knowledge that this stranger's power is so great that it can't be contained in one country, but right now, I'm glad. That is, if he's not the one behind the kidnapping. *How the hell can I know for sure?*

Belevich can say that my father and Jericho respect each other, but what if he's wrong? Am I willing to bet

Jericho's life on Belevich's word when I can't figure out why he knows so much about what's going on?

And what if this is all some kind of trap? What if Belevich is setting me up . . . and Jericho? He says his angle is to curry favor with my father, but I'm not sure what to believe anymore.

"What could he do to help?" I ask. The only thing I can do right now is gather as much information quickly, so that I can make this life-or-death decision as intelligently as possible. *Play the man, not the game.* My poker maxim applies here too.

"Last I knew, Federov had many Interpol agents on his payroll. They can access the security system at the hotel and find out who took him. And that is just the start of it."

The walls of the tiny break room feel like they're closing in on me as Belevich speaks. *My father has Interpol agents on his payroll?*

"How would we even get in touch with him?" I ask. "It's not like I have his phone number."

Belevich smiles and slides his phone from his pocket before holding it up. "But I do."

With eyes that feel like they're bugging out of my head, my gaze darts between Belevich's face and the phone. "You have my father's number. On your phone. As in, you could call him anytime?"

Belevich nods slowly.

He knows way more than he's telling me.

I bolt out of my chair and back away from him, reaching out behind me for the door frame. "Who the fuck are you? Are you one of his henchmen? You told me not to attract attention from the Bratva guys in the hotel, but how the fuck do I know you're not even worse?"

Belevich turns in his chair and throws an arm over the back, watching me with a raised eyebrow like he's amused that I'm two seconds from running.

"You can trust me or not, Indy. But you need to decide fast. Every moment we delay, there may be less of your husband for you to collect."

My stomach revolts at the image his words conjure —Jericho broken and bleeding somewhere—but I force it down because I can't handle even picturing it. Since the moment I first saw Jericho Forge, he's been the very definition of larger than life. Untouchable. Practically immortal. I can't stand, even for a second, to picture him hurt or in danger.

If he dies, it will break me.

The absolute truth rises up from the deepest part of my soul. I'm in love with Jericho Forge, and there's no way in hell I'm going to let him die before I get a chance to tell him that. Whatever I have to pay, barter, or bargain to get him back, *I will do it.*

"Call my father. Call him right now."

"As you wish." Belevich taps the screen on his phone and lifts it to his ear.

He speaks in Russian for a few moments while I hold my breath, wondering if I've made the wrong choice. *But what other choice did I really have?* None.

I wait for Belevich to offer the phone to me, so I can speak to this stranger who is my father, but instead, he finishes the short conversation and hangs up.

My eyes lock on his face. "What? What's going on? Doesn't he want to talk to me? Who the fuck did you really call?" Distrust batters at my insides, and I wish I had Goliath's gun in my hand at that very moment to threaten Belevich to get the truth.

"Calm down. He will speak to you soon."

I wrap my hand around the doorjamb and my entire body tenses, poised to bolt at the first possible sign that he has somehow screwed me over. "What the hell does that mean? He's calling you back?"

Belevich shakes his head as my mind races. "No. He's already here. In Prague. For you."

My heartbeat thunders in my ears, and static makes the hair on the back of my neck stand on end as I try to make sense of what he said.

My father is in Prague. For me.

"What? Why? Why the fuck would he be here?"

I take a step back, jerking my gaze off Belevich for a second to scan the silent hallway, as if I'm afraid the bogeyman is going to reach out from behind me and drag me away.

Belevich rises from the chair. "Federov says he

came to watch you play in the grand prix. I did not see him, otherwise I would have told you before. But like you, my attention was on the game, not the crowd."

He could be lying to me. All of this could be bullshit. He could have just called in a Russian hit squad to take out me and Goliath to finish the job they started in the hotel.

My jaw sets as I shake my head. "I don't trust you."

Belevich studies my face. "At this point, it does not matter whether you trust me or not. I have no ill will toward you or Forge."

"Do you work for my father?" I bite out the question.

It's the only explanation that could possibly make sense. Why else would Belevich help me? Why else would he have his number? How else could he have known about Summer? He must have some inside connection he hasn't disclosed.

Before Belevich can reply, shoes squeak against the linoleum, and I whip around to see Dr. Novotny in the hallway. I jump back from the doorway into the hall, not wanting to get trapped inside the break room.

She doesn't say anything about my abrupt movements, just sweeps a curious look over my tense form before speaking. "Your friend is going to be fine. He will need to be careful with his shoulder for a while, and while the pain will not be pleasant, he will heal."

I study her face for signs that she's lying—eye

movement, shifting of her head position, heavier breathing, unusual stillness—but I don't see any of them.

"You're sure?" I ask, still not certain if I want to believe her completely, because I haven't seen Goliath emerge from the treatment room yet.

"Yes. He was very lucky." She glances at Belevich. "Now you need to go. All of you."

"We cannot go yet," Belevich replies, stepping toward us.

"Why not?" Dr. Novotny snaps.

"Because Grigory Federov is on his way to meet his long-lost daughter."

Dr. Novotny stills for a few beats before whipping her head to the side to look at me, wide-eyed. "*This* is Illyana Federov?" Her jaw hangs slack as she scans me from head to toe.

The name sounds completely foreign as I repeat it in my head. *Illyana.*

"Yes, and I'm sure you will have his gratitude for assisting her," Belevich adds.

She seems to gather herself, wiping away the traces of shock. "Fine. I will clean up, but you must leave as soon as possible. I do not want to attract more attention than we already have. This neighborhood has eyes everywhere. There is no telling how many people have already seen your fancy car outside, and who they have told."

"Thank you, Marina. I'm in your debt."

"Indeed you are. I hope you live long enough to repay it, Mitri."

With her ominous statement, Dr. Novotny retreats from the room, leaving Belevich and me alone . . . waiting for Grigory Federov to arrive.

INDIA

*T*he next ten minutes seem to last an eternity, but eventually someone raps on the locked back door of the clinic.

In the treatment room, I take a step toward Goliath, who checks the screen of his phone and shoves it into his pocket. I keep praying he'll say he got a message from Jericho, but there hasn't been one yet. He looks a little unsteady as he rises to his feet with a makeshift sling cradling his left arm, but even in his banged-up state, his right hand shifts to the gun tucked into his pants. He's my only friend here, and the one thing I regret is not being able to get him alone so we could discuss what our plan B is if my decision blows up in our faces.

I keep asking myself—*what would Jericho do?* The

only answer I can come up with is stick to Goliath like he's my last hope for survival, which he very well might be.

Belevich's voice comes from the hallway, and a much deeper, gruffer voice replies in what I assume is Russian. *Why didn't I learn Russian?* Oh, wait, that's right, because I didn't know that I *was* Russian.

The deeper voice has to be my father's. Or at least, the man who claims to be my father.

I've never been so unsure of what to do in my life since the day I realized Summer and I were on our own for good because our mother wasn't coming back for us.

The soles of shoes slap against the linoleum floor, and I straighten my shoulders as if preparing for battle. The only choice I have is to meet whatever fate my decisions have brought head-on.

If it brings Jericho home to me, that's all that matters.

I remind myself for the hundredth time in the last ten minutes that Jericho liked my father enough to do business with him, and I'm hoping it wasn't a huge mistake to contact the man. Jericho would want me to stay safe. *And I want to have an army at my back to save him.* If this is what it takes to get that army, then so be it.

As Goliath and I wait in the treatment room, I find myself wishing we'd chosen somewhere with a second door, so we could escape if we needed to run. *Why didn't I plan an escape route? Why didn't he?*

Before I can answer that question, a man appears in the doorway.

As soon as his gaze lands on me, his craggy features soften enough to change his entire countenance from stony and forbidding to mortal man.

"Illyana." He whispers the Russian name that I never knew was mine as he crosses himself like he's in church. "You are the image of your mother." He presses a giant fist to his mouth as he stares at me with tears gathering in his eyes.

But his statement is completely wrong. "You're mistaken. I look nothing like my mother," I tell him, slipping behind Goliath's shoulder.

Federov's features harden beneath his steel-gray hair, and the tears are blinked away like they never existed.

"That bitch, Nina, wasn't your mother. Nina *took you from me.* She wanted to hurt me in the most painful way, and she did. I have waited years for this moment. She stole your life from you. She stole a lifetime from *us.* May she rot in hell where I sent her." His harsh tone punctuates every word with a growl.

Disbelief settles over me like a cold shroud, and my mouth drops open into an *o.* The beats of my heart come slower, pounding in my ears. My tongue sticks to my teeth as my mouth goes dry.

Nina was the name we were never supposed to call my mother, for a reason she never explained.

"What do you mean . . . Nina wasn't my mother?"

Federov bares his teeth and looks skyward, hauling in a deep breath that expands his barrel-like chest. He holds it for a moment before releasing it and focusing on me once more.

"Your mother, *Irina*, passed away a week before that bitch took you. Nina wanted to leave me with *nothing* after I cast her out."

I press my dry lips together and try to make sense of what the hell he's saying. It's not the thick accent making him difficult to comprehend, but an entire life's worth of lies.

"Who . . . who was Nina then?" *Nina wasn't my mother.* My breathing turns shallow as I grapple with the truth.

His nostrils flare like a bull sighting a red cape. "My mistress, to my lifelong regret."

Oh. My. God.

The heartbeat thudding in my ears grows louder. *The woman I've always thought was my mother . . . was my father's mistress.* Which means . . .

Summer isn't my sister.

I stare at him, stricken with the realization. "She . . ." I try to form a sentence, but I'm at a loss. I don't know what to say. What to think. What to feel.

How is this possible? This can't be possible.

But there's no sign that Federov is deceiving me. He watches me as I open my mouth again and again, probably gaping like a fish. Finally, he takes pity on me and explains.

"Nina was a vengeful woman, and I will never be able to beg your forgiveness for what I let happen. You were vulnerable because of me, Illyana. It was my fault she took you. But I have never stopped searching for you, even after they told me you were dead."

The room spins around me as I grapple with his confession. Goliath claps a hand on my shoulder to stop me from tipping over.

"Illyana, please. Sit down. You are . . . pale." Federov's rugged features shift to concerned.

I've been wrestling with this changing reality since finding out that I have a father, but this . . . this is more than I can handle.

My breathing continues to quicken, and I force it to slow. *Focus, Indy. Focus on what matters—Jericho. Everything else can wait.*

The only thing I care about right now is getting my husband back safely. I take all the information—about my father, his mistress, and my sister—and I shove it into a little box deep inside me and slam the lid shut. Straightening my shoulders, I meet my father's blue gaze, which looks uncannily like mine. *No. Don't think about that.*

I lift my chin higher. "I need your help. Jericho was

taken. I need you to help me get him back." I'm proud my statements come out sounding authoritative rather than trembling like my hands as I clench them into fists.

Federov's lips press together in a hard line, and for a moment, I fear he won't agree. *He's not allowed to say no.*

"Before you say anything, you should know this—if you want any hope of a relationship with me, you will help me right now. If you don't, then this moment is all you'll ever have to remember me by, because I'll disappear and you'll never see me again."

His chin lifts in a gesture that mimics my own, like he's not used to taking orders or being given ultimatums.

Too bad, Dad. I don't have time to waste, and if you don't help me, I'll find another way.

"And if I help get Forge back for you . . . you will spend time with me? Let me get to know the woman who is my daughter?"

There's nothing I wouldn't promise to get Forge back, but I have to know he's sincere.

"You get one shot with me. Don't make me regret this."

I wonder if I should feel bad about my ruthless request, but I can't summon the feelings necessary for that. This day has been a roller coaster of emotions, and the only way I'll be able to sleep again someday without nightmares about what I saw today is with Jericho by my side.

They say you don't truly appreciate what you have until it's gone, and every vibrating nerve in my body tells me that I'm not prepared to lose my husband. Not now. Not when I've finally admitted to myself that I'm in love with him. And the thought of being doomed to living a life without him . . . I couldn't bear it.

"*Please,*" I say as my father watches me in silence. "Please help me."

"It will be done," Federov says with a sharp nod.

He turns to a man beside him, one I hadn't even bothered to look at, and barks out something in Russian. The pale blond replies and disappears from the doorway. In the hallway, I can hear the echo of him speaking to someone on the phone.

"We will leave now," Federov says. "This neighborhood is not safe enough for you. I have somewhere else we can go. It is much more comfortable."

I glance up at Goliath and study the hard line of his jaw. He's staring at my father, not at me. I nudge him with an elbow to get his attention.

"Are you good with that?" I ask.

Goliath's dark gaze cuts from my father to me. "Forge would want you as safe as possible."

"And that is one thing we will always agree on," my father says.

Belevich speaks from the hallway, where he's been

listening to the entire conversation. "I agree. We should leave. It will be safer for Marina if we go."

"Okay," I say, agreeing mostly because I don't want to drag an innocent person into this, especially after she went above and beyond by helping us. "Then let's go."

*T*he more comfortable place Grigory Federov takes us is locked up like a vault. Actually, it's on *top* of a vault.

"I own this bank and the building," he says as he uses his thumbprint to unlock an elevator to take us to the top floor of a historic building.

Like Goliath, I'm checking for every available exit, because that's what Jericho would want me to do. *Stay safe at all costs.*

Belevich opted not to accompany us, and part of me freaked out when he hopped in the G-Wagen at the curb in front of the vet's office.

"You don't need me anymore," he said. "I'll see you another time, Indy. Better circumstances, one would hope."

If he set me up, I will stop at nothing to hunt him

down and exact retribution. I'm praying it doesn't come to that.

As soon as we step out of the elevator into a luxurious marble entryway leading to carved wooden doors that span farther than the width of my wingspan, Federov keys in a long code and scans his thumb again to open the door.

"Do you have security concerns?" I ask, wondering if the biometric devices are normal for him, or if there's an unknown threat I need to be worrying about. Basically, I'm second-guessing everything.

"I have good security so that there is no need for concern," he replies as he waves us inside.

Fair enough.

My heels click on the marble floors, and I try to keep my jaw from dropping as I take in the apartment we've entered. It's ornate, like something you'd see in a magazine. All gold gilt and white, and the furnishings and fixtures look like they must have cost a mint. The delicate decor looks nothing like I would have expected of the bull of a Russian who is my father.

No one greets us. The apartment is silent as he ushers us into a sitting room so large it houses three different seating arrangements. He walks toward the one farthest from the windows.

"Sit," he orders.

"My dress," I say, pointing at the bloodstains. I don't

want to sit on one of the white-and-gold damask sofas and ruin it.

Federov shakes his head. "I could replace it a hundred times and never notice the money gone. What does furniture matter when my daughter needs a place to sit?"

I guess, when you put it like that . . .

"Thanks." I take a seat on the expensive fabric and meet his gaze as he sits across from me. "How are we getting Jericho back? Do you have an army somewhere? Because that's where my head's at."

The Russian laughs, and it bounces off the ceilings fitted with intricate crown molding and gold-and-crystal chandeliers. "You are truly your father's daughter. But no, we do not strike with a sledgehammer when stealth would be more effective. I have put out word that I'm willing to pay for information and his return."

I blink, not sure I'm hearing him correctly. "You're going to ransom him back? That's your grand plan?"

His chin dips. "It seems most expedient, does it not?"

"What if the kidnappers don't want money?"

Federov makes a clucking sound with his tongue. "Everyone has a price, and I have enough money to pay even the steepest one. If he is alive, I will get him back for you."

If he is alive. I want to snatch those words from the air and shove them back in his mouth.

"He's alive, dammit. Don't you dare say that again."

Fear at the possibility of losing Jericho stabs me through the heart, and my voice shakes as I make the proclamation. Until this moment, I haven't dared consider the possibility that he might not be alive and waiting for rescue. *No. He's alive, goddammit.*

My father nods, albeit patronizingly. "All will be well. While we wait, are you hungry? Thirsty? What can I get you?"

My stomach revolts at the thought of eating, but I'm definitely not turning down a bracing shot with a chaser of water.

"Whiskey and water. Separately." I glance back to Goliath where the bodyguard stands like a sentinel behind me, despite his blood loss and injury. I motion for him to sit down, but he shakes his head. "Do you want anything?"

"Water."

Federov waves a hand to one of his goons, and I finally take stock of them. One is bald and solid, with rolls in the back of the neck that I see as he leaves the room to do my father's bidding. The other is almost as tall, but leaner, and his hair is so blond, it looks white. His posture is rigid, and his icy eyes survey me like I'm on display at a museum. I can't help but wonder how long they've known more about who I am than I did.

"Sir, you should sit," my father says to Goliath.

"You will be no good to my daughter or Forge if you collapse."

Goliath says nothing in response to my father's order and continues standing.

"Your choice. Not the smart one, though." Federov returns his attention to me. "Would you like to see a picture of your mother?"

His question catches me off guard and shakes my compartmentalization enough to let the shock from earlier sweep over me. I've been reunited with my long-lost father, learned my mother wasn't my mother, my sister isn't my sister, and we're awaiting news about my kidnapped husband with my almost-murdered bodyguard.

What I really want to do is curl up on the couch and indulge in a good long cry, but that's not going to help anything. Besides, I won't let myself shed a tear in front of these people. I refuse to show any weakness.

Shoving all those feelings back, I reply with a clipped, "Sure."

Federov reaches into his jacket pocket and withdraws a battered leather wallet. He flips it open and pulls out a photograph with tattered edges that looks like he's been carrying it for decades.

His crony returns with a tray and sets two shot glasses and waters on the glass-topped table between us before passing a bottled water to Goliath. Over the drinks, Federov holds out the picture.

As soon as my stare locks on the photo, I reach for the whiskey and toss back the entire shot with one gulp.

Holy shit. She looks just like me.

"Oh my God," I whisper, my hand shaking as I reach to take it from him.

"You are her image. She was the most beautiful woman I've ever seen, and so kind. Much too kind for a man like me."

I look up at his self-deprecating words and read the pain and regret in his gaze. "Because you had a mistress."

"Yes. Irina deserved a prince among men, but she fell in love with a brute. I was too selfish to try to change her mind."

"What . . . what happened to her?" I choke on the question and snatch the water to wash down the lump in my throat.

"Cancer. We caught it much too late. She was too young to be taken, or so I thought. I would have given everything to save her, but there was no time. She faded before my eyes in mere weeks."

"How could you have cheated on her if you loved her so much?"

His remorseful expression hardens. "I told you, I did not deserve Irina. I have accepted my punishment for over two decades. My penance is not one I would wish on any other man. But still, I repented too late."

"And my . . ." I swallow and stop myself from saying *mother.* "Nina . . . she took me from you."

"Yes." His reply is clipped as he reaches for a shot glass of clear liquid that I assume is vodka.

"You thought I was dead."

His mouth tenses as he presses the glass to it, and he gives me a nod before tossing it back.

"How would you know that? What made you think that?"

Federov's gaze drops and his jaw rocks from side to side. "We found Nina. Many years ago. She swore you were dead. The circumstances under which she swore made me believe she was telling the truth."

My lower lip trembles as I listen to what he's not saying. They found her. Took her. And . . . "How did you make her talk? Did you . . . torture her?" *Another image I don't want to picture.*

Federov's gaze shifts to the window where streetlights illuminate the hard lines of his face. "She stole the only thing left that mattered to me. She deserved no mercy." His blue gaze comes back to me. "But she lied even then, and I left you with no one to care for you at all."

His regret is impossible to miss in the emotion-drenched words.

"Not for long. Alanna found us, and she was more of a mother to me than I had ever known. I will never approve of what you did, but I can't say I wouldn't do some unforgivable things to help find Jericho faster."

The older man's shoulders relax, and he looks like I've given him a stay of execution. But really, I'm focusing on the only thing I care about right now. *Where are you, Jericho? Come back to me.*

The burn of the whiskey turns to heat in my belly.

"When will we hear something?" I ask. "I can't just sit here and do nothing."

Federov points to the blond man. "When we hear something, his phone will ring. We must be patient."

Patient is the last thing I want to be, but what other choice do I have?

Taking a slow breath to calm my racing heart, I decide to use this time to find answers to the questions that have been plaguing me. "How did you know I was alive? What made you start looking again if you thought I was dead?"

Goliath shifts behind me, and I'm not sure if it's because he's growing weaker, or if he's just as interested in hearing the answer as I am.

Federov lifts his glass in the air over his shoulder, and the bald goon disappears for a moment and returns with a bottle of vodka to splash another measure into it. My father tips it back like he's drinking water. When he replaces it on the table with a click, he meets my gaze.

"Your . . . Summer." He almost said *sister* but changed his mind at the last minute.

No. I'm not going to let him take that from me.

"My *sister*, you mean." I sit up straighter on the sofa as I correct him. "Because that's exactly what she is. It doesn't matter if we don't share blood. That's not what makes someone family. Family is being there for each other and never walking away. Family means sacrificing for one another."

A muscle ticks in Federov's jaw. "Your *family* is fond of using your name to get ahead."

"You can't tell me anything about Summer that's going to surprise me anymore. She fucked up. She knows she fucked up. I'm not disowning her."

He watches me carefully, like every word I speak is gold-plated. "No, I would not either. In fact, if not for her using your name and getting taken, I would never know that you were still alive."

My fingers curl into the edge of the sofa cushion. "What do you mean? How does that add up? I don't understand."

"Belevich."

As soon as he says the Russian poker player's name, my jaw goes slack. *I fucking knew he had inside information.*

"What does he have to do with this?" I grit the words out from between clenched teeth.

"His father was a friend. His whole family has been to my home in Russia, and when Dmitri was there, he saw a picture of Irina in my office. It hangs over my fireplace. When he saw you in a shop in Ibiza, he contacted me, saying he'd seen her double. I could not believe it. But when I had you investigated, I had hope for the first time in many years that we would be reunited. But somehow . . . word got out. I had a leak in my organization."

Belevich is the one who started all of this. That motherfucker. He could have told me. *Why didn't he?*

"When the hell was this?" I demand.

"Not long before they took your sister, thinking she was you. They ransomed her back to me, telling me she was you."

Belevich knew when we played at La Reina. He knew why I was playing. He knew Summer had been kidnapped because they thought she was me. *And he said nothing.* He and I have a score to settle.

I drop my gaze to the empty whiskey glass and wish for it to refill magically. When it doesn't, I look up at Federov.

"They really took Summer because they thought she was me?"

His blue eyes are solemn. "Yes. Because they knew I would pay anything to get you back."

"But . . . Jericho is the one who got Summer back." I press two fingers to my temple as it throbs with the beginning of a massive headache from trying to process all this information.

"I asked him for a favor. But I did not know the

kidnappers learned the woman they held wasn't you. They tried to ransom her to both you and to me after that. Forge learned who the girl was to you without telling me either. And then he pulled his biggest trick of all." Federov pauses, and I know what he's going to say.

Jericho made his bargain with me.

"He married you."

Right now, in this moment when my spark of love has grown into a raging inferno, isn't the time I want to remember that Jericho married me under false pretenses. *It doesn't matter. Does it?* Because this isn't about a deal anymore. This is *real*.

A tendril of doubt curls in my chest, but I mentally brush it away.

"He married me to protect me," I say, conviction reinforcing my words.

"He did it for an advantage in business. For leverage," my father says, contradicting me. "But . . . when I saw him after, I wondered if it was still only business. I did not believe a man could stay hard-hearted against a daughter of my blood. I have been in his position. I couldn't give up Irina, even though she deserved a better man. Forge and I are cut from the same cloth. We take what we want, for our own reasons, and will never apologize for it."

His comparison is the last thing I want to hear. I shake my head. "I don't want to talk about that right now."

I grip the tumbler of water tightly, because if I give in to the million other questions on my mind, I'll lose focus on what matters—Jericho.

Glancing up at the blond man, I ask, "Can't you get an update? I don't want to wait here all night, wondering what the hell is going on. We have to do something."

I drop the photo on the table in front of me, even though part of me wants to keep it. Federov grasps it, presses a kiss to the worn paper, and tucks it away in his wallet.

"Kostya." He turns to look at the man behind him and gives an order in Russian.

The blond, who must be Kostya, makes a phone call.

The room goes silent except for harsh sounds of a language I've never wanted to understand more. When Kostya hangs up, he says something to Federov that causes my father to rise and bite out a terse response. Kostya replies and turns to leave, clearly having been given his marching orders.

"What? What's going on?"

With a glower settling over his face, my father speaks through gritted teeth. "We have a lead."

"What kind of lead?" I jerk my gaze from him to Goliath and back again. "Is he okay? Where is he? Who has him?"

"Someone who says they want a hundred million dollars in exchange for his return."

FORGE

I wake to the coppery tang of blood in my mouth and the scent of raw meat. The incessant thundering in my head tells me I'm not dreaming. *But I'm not dead either.*

My shoulders burn, and my arms feel like they're being pulled from the sockets, dragged down by my body weight. The zip ties bite into my wrists, and my exposed skin drips with condensation as the cool air lowers my core temperature.

I've faced worse.

It takes a hell of a lot more to kill a man like me, and tonight, I refuse to fucking die.

Someone sold me out. I don't know who and I don't know how, but if I get out of here . . . *No, not if. When.*

From behind me, a door creaks, and shoes squeak on the floor of the meat locker as someone approaches. I relax as much as possible, wanting to preserve any advantage I might have by appearing to be unconscious.

"Boss? Boss."

The whispered word, *in English*, in a voice I recognize, has me jerking my head around. *Koba.* My suspicions about him roar to the forefront of my brain.

Is he with them? Coming to kill me? But if he were, why would he be whispering?

Only one way to find out.

"Get me down. Hurry," I say, snapping out the order.

The squeaking footsteps come closer, and I pray to anyone who will listen that he's not here to stab me in the back, and is only making himself known so that I'll be aware of who killed me.

I brought him to Prague to keep an eye on him. *Keep your friends close and your enemies closer.*

That decision could be my downfall.

Instead of a knife between my shoulder blades, he slices through the zip ties binding my feet. I stretch them out and try to touch the floor, but I can't reach.

"I followed them. I was in the stairwell when they carried you out. I hid behind a fire door on the floor below and had to wait for them to leave. There's only one here right now."

The story sounds like it could be true, but I'm not exactly in the most trusting mood at present.

"My arms. Hurry up."

Cold steel touches my skin as Koba cuts the plastic

bindings, and as soon as they break, I fall into him as my knees give way when my feet hit the floor. Koba grips my shoulders, and thousands of invisible pins and needles jab into me as blood rushes back into my limbs. Clenching my teeth, I try to steady my legs.

"Fuck. You okay, boss?" Koba whips the bag off my head.

Thank fuck. I blink in the dim light of the room, and the black spots finally disappear from my vision.

"Fine. Time to get the fuck out of here."

Koba's head bobs. "I got a car outside, in the alley across the street. We just have to make it there."

"Gun?" I ask, partly because I need a way to fight back, and partly to see if he's willing to give me one. If he's working against me, he wouldn't free me and then arm me.

When he pulls a pistol from his waistband and offers it to me, I make a snap decision. I was wrong. Koba isn't here to kill me. His next words seal it.

"I only have one. Would've shot them when they were taking you, but I didn't want to risk—"

"Doesn't matter. Let's go."

"This way." Koba leads me out of the cooler, palming a knife at his side. He presses against the door, opening it slowly.

I probably should offer to give the gun back because he's in the lead, but there's no way in hell I want to be unarmed. Not now.

"Clear," he whispers, and together we move out of the cooler down a dingy concrete hallway.

I have no fucking clue where we are, but my mind is fixed on what needs to happen right now. *Get the fuck out of here. Get back to Indy. Make sure she's safe. Get us the fuck out of this country.*

Those are my priorities, in order.

Together, we creep down the hall, and my arms and shoulders protest with every sweep of the gun. Up ahead is a set of double doors. When we reach them, Koba pauses.

"Through here, there's another hallway, and on the right, there's a room where they were holed up. The door to the outside isn't far beyond it."

"Got it. Let's move."

The double doors open on shrieking hinges, and if there's a single person in the vicinity, there's no way they could miss it. The scrape of a chair against concrete is the next sound I hear, and Koba and I lock eyes.

"Run," we both say, and we bolt like sprinters off the line.

We pass the doorway he described just as a man appears in it, gun drawn.

I raise the pistol and fire, and he staggers backward as the bullets pierce his chest. Someone else yells, but I focus on the door only a dozen feet away. *Freedom.* As soon as I reach it, I kick it open.

Gunshots erupt, and Koba jumps in front of me to

throw the knife he carries. It catches the second shooter in the throat, but not before another deafening barrage of bullets explode from the barrel.

"Get down!" I yell as I fire back, but it's too late.

Koba hits the floor, the life already leaving his eyes as the door swings shut, trapping us both inside.

Fuck. Fuck. I drop to a knee beside him, but Koba shakes his head when I lift him.

"No. Just go. Go." The words come out as a gurgle. *Death rattle.*

I adjust my grip, but blood trickles from the corner of his mouth as his stare goes blank.

Fuuuck.

"Goddammit." I squeeze his hand and make a decision that guts me. *I have to leave him.* "I'll get you home to your family. Somehow."

Rising to my feet, I shoulder the door open and run outside, praying there aren't any more of them waiting outside. My prayers go unanswered as a gunshot cracks through the darkness. I fire back at the muzzle flash, and the gunfire stops.

Wherever we are, it's the dead of night, and the moon offers only the dimmest light. I rush across the street, which is empty, and duck behind the corner of a brick building.

More gunfire erupts from the building I just escaped.

I need to find the fucking car. Otherwise, I'm a dead man walking. Following nothing but my instincts, I run along the side of the building and look for the alley Koba described.

I won't let your death be in vain.

I reach the opposite end of the wall and spot a dark sedan. In a sprint, I rush to the driver's door and climb inside. The keys are in the ignition.

Thank fuck.

I fire up the engine and throw it in gear. The tires squeal as I punch the gas. With the headlights off, I haul ass down the alley and turn the corner to reach the road. A muzzle flash comes from directly in front of me just before bullets hit the windshield. It breaks, but the safety glass keeps it from shattering in my face.

I flip on the headlights and floor the accelerator. *You shot at the wrong guy, motherfucker.*

He lays down more fire, and bullets punch through the car as I careen toward him. He tries to run, but he's too slow. With a thump, I slam into him from behind and his body bounces up on the hood, his face pressing against the spiderwebbed windshield.

I put the car in reverse, expecting another hail of bullets, but none come. I throw the car in park and jump out.

It might cost me my life, but if I live, I need to know who the fuck to hunt down for this, or neither Indy or I will ever be able to go a day without looking over our shoulders. That's not a life I want for her.

I drag the man's body off the car and crouch over it.

He's as dead as he'll ever be, and I feel no shame or recrimination as I dig through his pockets, taking his wallet, his phone, and his gun. With a backward glance at the warehouse, I dart to the driver's door and slide inside.

Squinting to see through the demolished windshield, I shift gears and punch the accelerator.

I'm coming, Ace. Nothing is going to keep me from you. Now, where the hell are you?

*K*ostya continues making calls, trying to find information about where Jericho is being held, and Goliath and I wait in strained silence.

After the marathon of a day playing poker and the shock that followed, I'm starting to droop, but there's no way in hell I'm closing my eyes for even a second. Not until we have something concrete. I stifle a yawn as my clutch vibrates.

No. Not my clutch. My phone.

Kidnappers? Maybe trying to ransom him to me while they wait for an answer from Federov?

Goliath's attention cuts from my father and his men to me as I snap open the clutch and stare at the screen of my phone.

It reads UNKNOWN NUMBER.

Chills skitter down my spine, just like they did every time Summer's kidnappers called.

"What is it? Who is calling?" Federov asks.

With my heart hammering, I flash the screen at him.

"I will answer," he says.

I shake my head. "I can do this."

With a shaking finger, I tap the screen and lift the phone to my ear. "Hello?"

"Sweet fucking Christ, I needed to hear your voice."

The connection crackles and the words cut out, but every hair on my body stands on end.

"Jericho? Oh my God. Is that you?"

The phone goes silent, and I yank it away from my ear to stare at the screen. CALL FAILED.

"No!"

"Was it Forge?" Federov asks, reaching across the table for the phone, but I clutch it to my chest.

My gaze darts from the phone to him and back again. "I think so," I whisper. My heart hammers as I question myself. *Was it him? It was him. Right?*

It vibrates again, and I answer it on the first ring.

"Jericho?"

"Yeah, Ace. It's me."

"Thank God." Sweet relief, the likes of which I've never known, settles over me, and everyone else in the room seems to hold their breath as I talk. "Are you okay? Where are you? Are you safe?"

As soon as I rattle off the questions, Jericho

laughs, and with every second, I fear the call will drop again. I bite down on my lip as my eyes burn with tears.

"That's what I was going to ask you."

"I'm fine. I'm . . . with my father and Goliath. We left the hotel, but we're safe. Where are you?"

"Trying to get to you. I thought G was dead. Thank fuck, he's not."

"The others . . ." My voice shakes as I try to tell him. I swallow and spit it out. "They're dead."

"I heard shots before they knocked me out." Jericho's tone sounds just as grim as mine. "Koba is too."

I sit up straighter. "How? He disappeared from the hotel. We thought . . . We thought he was part of it."

"He saved me. Didn't make it out. But that's all for later. Right now, the only thing that matters is getting to you. Can I talk to Goliath for a second? We need a plan."

The last thing in the world I want to do is give up that phone, but if it gets me what I want most—to see Jericho, safe and sound—I'll do it.

"Okay. Here he is." I hand the phone off, and Goliath speaks in a language I don't recognize.

Why hadn't I asked Jericho what it was the first time I heard it? How many languages does my husband speak?

From the corner of my eye, I can see my father staring at Goliath, and it's clear from his clenched hands and stiffened posture that he doesn't speak the language either and hates being at a disadvantage.

The conversation is short, and Goliath hands the phone back to me only thirty seconds later.

"Ace?"

"I'm here." My heart swells with joy just hearing his voice, but I try to tamp it down. I need to see him. Touch him. Hug him. Then I'll believe he's really okay.

"Goliath is going to have your father bring you to the private air strip where we landed. Stick close to him. Don't leave his side. We're getting the hell out of Prague."

"Okay," I say, my voice shaking enough that there's no way Jericho misses it.

"I'll see you soon. I promise. Everything's going to be okay, Ace." His voice is filled with confidence, and I want to believe him.

The words *I love you* hover on my lips, but I can't get them out, because something in me wants to say them to him in person and watch his face as he hears. Not in a room full of men staring at me on the phone. As soon as I hang up, I regret that I didn't say them.

What if I never get the chance?

I won't think about that. Not now. The only thing that matters is getting to him.

I shoot to my feet and meet my father's gaze. "We need a ride."

FORGE

*H*earing Indy's voice isn't enough. I need to have her in my arms on the plane home before I'll be able to breathe easy. I punch in the address of the airport in the GPS on the phone I stole from Yuri Pallovich, if the name on the license in the wallet I stole off the dead guy is real.

I've spent time in Prague, but I don't know this maze of streets well enough to navigate them without assistance. The airport is only thirty minutes away, and according to Goliath, it shouldn't take them much longer to get there, if he's right about where they are. I would put money on Goliath being right, because the man has an uncanny sense of direction and can navigate a ship without radar through a narrow channel in the densest fog known to man. I would trust him with my life, and right now, I'm trusting him with Indy's.

"Get her to me. No matter what it takes," I told him in Afrikaans. It's the language of his homeland, and over the years, he taught me enough to get by with the basics. It had been vital more than once when we had to speak in front of others without being understood.

I turn left, backtracking my way through the city. I drove in a circle while I was talking to Indy and Goliath, in part because I took a wrong turn, and also because I wanted to make sure I wasn't being followed.

Thirty minutes. That's all that stands between me and seeing her safe again.

In the back of my mind, one name rumbles over and over.

Bastien de Vere. Bastien de Vere.

If he was behind this, my death by a thousand cuts is going to be reduced to one slice.

Across his throat.

"*T*his is not a good idea," my father says after I repeat the instructions Jericho gave Goliath and me.

I march to the door. "No disrespect, but I wasn't asking for your opinion. We need a ride to the airport."

My father's lips settle into a hard line, but I don't care if he's not used to being contradicted. The only thing that matters to me is getting to the airport as fast as humanly possible.

Silence hangs between us, and part of me expects him to say no, purely based on his stiff posture. But I refuse to back down. I didn't grow up on the streets, fending for myself and my sister, just to be cowed by any man, even if he is my father. I don't trust him, and if he ever wants to see me again, he needs to realize his actions right now will trump all his stories of regret.

"We're wasting time. Forge will be there. He expects his wife to be there as well," Goliath says, unable to bear the silence any longer.

"Forge—" Federov says, and I interrupt.

"Is my husband, and I'm going to him." I cross my arms over my chest. "We'll get there with or without you."

My father rises and walks toward me. "I should have known you would be as stubborn as me. Fine. We will go, and I will speak to Forge directly about my concerns for your safety."

Knock yourself out, I think. Because I don't care what he says once we get there. I just need to see Jericho in one piece.

"Thank you."

Federov's two security people flank him as he walks toward the door. The blond, Kostya, reaches it first, and I step aside so he can unlock and unbolt it before swinging it open.

The ride to the airport passes as slowly as hundred-year-old honey working its way down the side of a jar. Goliath flips between a text with someone I assume is Jericho and the GPS on the screen of his phone the entire time.

Does he expect them to try to take us somewhere else? As much as I want to be able to trust my father as he asks me question after question about my life, it's not an easy thing to do.

I just want to get back to Jericho and get the hell out of here.

That's when it hits me—I'm the reason Donnigan, Bates, and Koba are dead. I'm the reason Jericho was kidnapped. If I hadn't insisted on playing this grand prix, we wouldn't have been in such a vulnerable position.

This all happened because of me. Every single bit of it.

Guilt threatens to drag me under. If something happens to Jericho before he gets to the airport, I will never be able to forgive myself. Tears burn my eyes, and all I want to do is get to him.

I fidget in my seat, staring out the window, barely answering my father's questions. As we get closer, runway lights glow in the sky, and my hand is poised over the latch on my seat belt.

Lev, who I've learned is Kostya's bald counterpart, badges us through the gate and parks inside one of the hangars. Goliath opens the door of the SUV, and as soon as he is out of my way, I hit the ground running.

I've only taken two steps toward the jet before Goliath reaches out to grab my wrist. "That isn't Forge's plane."

I whip my head around to face my father as the other doors of the SUV slam shut.

"I said I'd bring you to the airport, not that I'd let you leave with him."

With my teeth bared, I stride toward him. "If you *ever* want to see me again, you won't stand in my way right now. You will *never* stand in my way when it comes to my family. Do you understand me?"

A slash of pain shoots across the old man's proud face before he can disguise it. "The Federov blood runs hot in your veins, just like mine. Do not shut me out of your life for wanting to keep you safe."

"I'm safe with Jericho." My tone leaves no room for argument.

My father opens his mouth to reply, but both Lev and Kostya raise their weapons and train them on the form of a man who steps into the shadows of the hangar.

It doesn't matter that I can't see him. I know exactly who it is.

"No! Put them down! If you shoot him, I'll gut you myself." The bloodthirsty threat comes from God only knows where, but one thing is certain—I hate having guns pointed at my husband.

Goliath takes a step forward, and I don't know what he's planning to do, but Federov says something in Russian. Both men lower their weapons partially as the man walks toward us, finally stepping into the light from the beams of the SUV's headlights.

Jericho. His face is dirty and blood streaked, but it's the most gorgeous face I've ever seen. *He's alive.*

I break into a sprint, racing toward the man I feared I'd never see again.

We collide in a crush of limbs, and his arms wrap around me so tightly that my lungs threaten to burst, but I don't care. I press my face to his chest and breathe in his scent. He's solid and real and *alive*.

"Thank God," I whisper.

"I'm so fucking happy to see you." His hands rise to my head, burying in my messy hair, and he pulls me back to stare into my eyes. "I thought . . ." His voice breaks off, and I shake my head.

"I'm fine. Totally fine. Other than a few years scared off my life."

He presses a kiss to my forehead. "I'm so sorry. This never should've—"

Before he can apologize more, I press my lips carefully against his bloodied ones to silence him. "I missed you," I whisper against his skin as I pull back a fraction.

Behind me, someone clears his throat, and I have the sudden urge to punch that person in the face. No one gets to interrupt this moment. *No one.*

But my father didn't get the memo.

"Forge, you have information or no?"

Instead of letting me go, Jericho pulls me against his body and wraps me tightly in his arms again before responding. His touch slows my racing heartbeat, and the tension I've been carrying melts away one drop at a time.

Finally, he replies. "I have information."

"Are you going to share it?"

"Should I?"

I can almost picture my father bristling at the question. I haven't known him more than a couple of hours, but it didn't even take ten minutes to realize the proud Russian's orders are always followed. Except, perhaps, by me. And apparently, Forge.

Before Federov can reply, a jet stops on the tarmac beyond the hangar, and wind whips my hair in every direction.

"Our ride's here, Ace," Jericho whispers in my ear. "Get on board with Goliath, and I'll be right behind you. There are a few things I'd like to say to your father."

I pull back and meet his turbulent gray gaze. "Shouldn't I be part of the discussion?"

Jericho tucks my wild hair behind one ear and leans forward to whisper. "There are a few things I need to know, but he may not answer in front of you. I promise I'll fill you in on everything as soon as we're airborne." He presses another kiss to my brow before he raises his head. "Trust me."

"Okay." When he releases me from his arms, I spin around to face my father. His features are set in stone as I walk toward him and hold out a hand. "Thank you for your help."

He clasps it between his two massive ones. "You're my daughter. There is nothing I wouldn't do for you . . . but I would prefer you come with me. Spend time with me. I would like to know you, Illyana."

"My name is Indy," I tell him. "And I want to go home. Everything else . . . we can talk about later."

He straightens, opening his mouth like he wants to argue, but then shuts it again. "If that is what you want, and Forge can assure me of your safety . . . then so be it."

Federov drops my hand and wraps me in a bear hug. The kind of a hug a grown daughter would receive from her father on her wedding day before he gave her away to another man. The kind that says *I love you and I don't want to let you go, but I must.*

When he releases me, his gaze tracks over my face as if memorizing it. Like it's the last time he'll ever see me.

"We'll talk . . . soon," I say, not sure why I'm trying to make him feel better.

His Adam's apple bobs as he steps away. "Thank you for summoning me for help. It was my honor."

With one last smile at the father I never knew I had, I turn and walk toward the jet.

*A*s soon as Indy is on board with Goliath, I pull the wallet out of my pocket and slide the ID out of the plastic protector. The guy couldn't have been much of a professional, because it should be the first rule of kidnapping for ransom that you don't bring your ID with you. But the name on it, Yuri Pallovich, matches the credit cards in the wallet. It's not like I got much of a look at his face when it was pressed against the windshield, so I don't know if it's stolen. I'm going to assume not.

"You know this guy?" I hold it out to Federov.

The older man snatches it from my grip and stares down at it. After he's done, he turns around to hold it out to a blond man and then the bald one. In Russian, they talk amongst themselves, but from the shaking of heads, they don't know him.

Federov confirms it. "We do not know him." The blond snaps a picture of the ID before handing it back to Federov, who offers it to me. "But we will find him."

"He's dead. I need you to find out who he works for."

Federov's chin lifts as he surveys me with new respect. "You killed him?"

"Him and others." I hold out the stolen phone, with the screen pulled up to show the map where I think the warehouse was. "You'll find bodies in a brick warehouse. One of them is my employee. Near the door. Shot in the chest. I would be grateful if you could help me get him and my two men from the hotel home."

The blond leans over Federov's shoulder to look at the map and points. "There are warehouses here. I know the area."

"Make the calls, Kostya. Maybe we will have more answers," Federov orders before meeting my gaze.

"Tell me what you find. I'll do the same," I say.

His expression shifts into the one he had when he sat across the desk from me, a stubborn negotiator, marking up the contract he'd already agreed to. "Agreed. But Illyana would still be safer in Russia."

"You don't know that." I shove the wallet and phone back in my pocket. "The threats could be related to you."

Federov's lower lip pushes outward. "If they were related to me, they would have taken Illyana, not you.

You cannot deny that you have your own enemies, Forge. From what I am told, Bastien de Vere is out for blood, when he never would've dared to hurt Illyana before. That is because of you."

His well-placed jab hits right where he intends, in my conscience. Bastien never would have hurt Indy before, but his MO with respect to her has changed completely now that she's my wife. First the chopper incident in Mallorca, and then drugs in the suitcase.

"I'll keep her safe."

Federov steps toward me, no doubt trying to intimidate, but I'm not one of his underlings. "You better, or I will make sure you never see her again. Do not cross me, Forge. I will not lose her when I've only just found her again."

"Tell me if you find anything. I'll be in touch." It's all I can manage before more oily guilt rushes back in.

"I will see her again soon. You will make it happen," Federov orders as I turn to walk to the jet.

I look sideways at him. "She'll see you if she wants to."

Federov points at me. "Make it happen, Forge."

I don't argue further with the old man. I've got more important things to do—like make sure no one touched a single hair on my wife's beautiful blond head before I get my revenge.

*J*ericho climbs aboard, and the flight attendant closes the door behind him. I'm a mess of emotions as he walks toward me. I struggle to find words, but none seem appropriate.

"I'm sorry," Jericho says when he sits next to me and clasps my hand between his bloodstained ones. "I'm so fucking sorry, Indy."

I rear back, staring at him in shock. "Why are you sorry? I'm the reason we were here. This is all on me. Koba, Bates, Donnigan . . ." I sniffle as the tears I've been holding back escape down my cheeks.

Jericho pushes up the armrest between our seats and pulls me against his side. "Ace, no. Don't think that. This isn't your fault."

"How is it not? I insisted on going. If I hadn't . . ."

"They would've gotten me some other way."

I shake my head. "No. I made us vulnerable. I put us in the open, made it easy for someone to do this. I never realized it would be so dangerous to leave the goddamned house."

A muscle in Jericho's jaw ticks, and he winces as if he's in pain.

"I'm right. You don't have to spare me to make me feel better. I'll never forgive myself for this."

"Don't," he says, hauling me onto his lap and pressing his face into my tangled hair. "This is on me, Ace. Not you. Or hell, maybe on your father. We don't know. When we find out who was behind it, we'll assign blame. But, this. Is. Not. Your. Fault." He presses a kiss to my face to punctuate each word. "It kills me to hear you say that."

My hands fist his shirt, and I stare into those fathomless gray eyes as my tears fall faster and harder until I'm sobbing. "I'm just so fucking glad you're okay. I . . . I was terrified. I thought . . . when I came off the elevator, and I saw those bodies . . . I thought I was going to find yours, and it was going to break me."

Jericho catches my tears on his thumbs, trying to wipe them away, but they come too fast. "Don't say that. Nothing could break you. You're the strongest woman I know. No matter what ever happens to me, you *will be fine.* Do you hear me?"

But he's wrong. He doesn't understand. I've fallen

completely and irrevocably in love with him, and if something had happened to him, I wouldn't be fine. Jericho Forge has become as necessary in my life as breathing. He gives me something I've never had before —acceptance.

I want to tell him how I feel, right here and now, but I'm a sobbing mess. When I tell him I'm in love with him, I don't want him to think I don't know what I'm saying.

What if you never get the chance? an insidious voice inside me whispers. *You never know which day will be your last. Or his last . . .*

I tell that voice to shut the hell up as I settle into my seat and clip my belt when the captain announces that we're taking off. The jet hurtles down the runway and up into the air moments later, but as soon as we level out, Jericho unhooks my seat belt and throws his arm around my shoulder to pull me against his side. He groans, and I jerk my chin up to look at the pain twisting his sharp features.

"What's wrong?"

"Nothing. I'm fine."

I scan his face, looking for every flinch of discomfort. "Truth. Now." When he tries to smile and cover it up, I add, "Please, Jericho. I can handle it."

"My head feels like it's been caved in, and my shoulders ache from being hung up by my wrists. I'll be fine, though."

"We need to get something for the pain." I pop to my feet before he can argue, and find the flight attendant. A few moments later, I return with a pill bottle. "Take these."

As I tap the tablets in his hand and then hold out a bottle of water, an image pops into my head of Jericho hanging from a hook, awaiting torture, and chills ripple over my body.

Thank God Koba helped him escape. I've never been so glad to be wrong about anyone as I was about him. If he hadn't helped . . . I don't even want to think about what could have happened.

But Jericho's fine. He's here. He's alive. I keep repeating that to myself until the chills dissipate. But after they do, another vision arises, and this time it's of the casualties from this tragedy.

"What about the—" I can't bring myself to say *bodies.* "Donnigan and Bates . . . and Koba?"

"I asked your father for help. We'll get them home."

From the lines settling deeper in Jericho's stubbled face, it's obvious that leaving the fallen behind is shredding him inside. Part of me wishes we could stay and take care of it ourselves, but I know we can't. Jericho wants to get me to safety first, and I want *him* safe, so I'm not going to argue.

Mindful of the injuries he told me about, when I sit back down beside him, I press my cheek gently against him. "I'm sorry. So sorry. I know they were your friends. Not just your employees."

"Thank you," he says, his voice rough with emotion.

I carefully rest against his chest, offering him whatever comfort I can. Eventually, I relax, listening to the steady rhythm of his heartbeat.

15

INDIA

I never stop touching him, not for a single minute of the flight home. I can't. I need to feel the heat of his skin and know that he's real. Know that he's safe. Know that he's *mine.*

He lifts me back onto his lap, neither of us speaking as he cups my head and keeps my ear pressed against his chest. When we touch down, I keep my fingers threaded through his, gripping tight, like I might lose him at any moment.

During the short helicopter ride to Isla del Cielo, I sit pressed against his side, his arm curled around my shoulders, and it still isn't enough. As we walk toward the house, I match my strides to his, and when we step over the threshold, I finally feel like I can breathe without a massive weight pressing down on my chest.

And still, I don't want to let him go.

I follow him to the bathroom, not asking for permission before I unbutton his torn shirt and help slide it carefully from his shoulders. I start the shower, and then strip out of my ruined dress and step inside the glass enclosure with him.

Under the hot spray, I gently wash him, letting the horrors of the prior day slip down the drain with the blood-tinged water. When I'm finished, Jericho reaches for a fresh washcloth and wordlessly does the same for me. Every stroke makes me feel precious and cherished, and so goddamned grateful that I have him back.

We both dry ourselves, and I follow him into the bedroom. When I stop by the bed, I turn to face him, my emotions raw. I drop the towel, baring myself to him, revealing a woman who needs to be reassured by the touch of her man.

"I need you. My hands on your body. Your taste on my lips. Your breath against my skin. I need to feel you. Feel that you're safe and everything's going to be okay." The words tumble out of me, and I don't even know if they make sense.

Jericho's gaze heats, and he strides toward me. On his face, I see the same ragged emotions reflected—lust, longing, and possessiveness. "Whatever you need, I'll give it to you."

"No, I want to give it to *you*."

He crosses the room and delves his hands into my hair, skimming them down my back as I memorize every plane of his body with my palms. Skin to skin, we slant our lips against each other's. One step at a time, I turn us until Jericho's legs hit the mattress.

His darkened gray gaze lifts to mine as I urge him to sit. His hands circle my waist as he brings me closer until I'm straddling his legs.

"The only thing I wanted was to get back to you. That's all that mattered." Jericho's voice is hoarse, and my heart clenches as I lower my forehead to his.

"There's nothing I wouldn't have done to get you back. *Nothing.*"

Moving slowly, I press kiss after kiss on his forehead, cheeks, nose, chin, and finally, his mouth again. Damp locks of my hair trail over his skin, and I lose track of time as I memorize his face with my lips.

When his grip tightens, I stare down into dark gray eyes filled with the same desperation overwhelming me.

"I need my wife."

"Yes," I whisper, my voice ragged and raw.

His hands close over my upper arms, and he guides me until his cock slides between the slick folds of my pussy. "You feel that? I'm real. Alive. And yours. Take me. I need to be inside you."

"God, yes." There's nothing I'd rather do more than worship him. *Show him how much I love him.*

Shifting on his hips, I slide against him, positioning the head against my entrance. His muscles twitch beneath me, and his reaction urges me on.

My tongue slides along his earlobe, and he inhales a sharp breath.

"You're the most beautiful man I've ever seen."

Covered in the stubble he can never seem to be rid of, his shadowed jaw shifts.

"You're far and away the most gorgeous and incredible woman I've ever known. I—"

"This is about you. Not me." I push down, taking half his cock inside me.

"I don't deserve you, Indy. Not for one single second." Jericho's words come out strangled.

"But you've got me anyway." I slide down the rest of the way, taking him balls deep.

His hand fists my damp hair, and his groans are music to my ears. He moves back on the bed until I'm kneeling over him.

"You're so fucking beautiful." He reaches up to stroke his knuckles along my cheek. "Ride me, Indy."

"It would be my pleasure."

I rise up and push down again, reveling in the ribbons of exquisite sensation that flutter through my body as his thick cock stretches me. There's nothing between us . . . except my fear that he'll never love me like I love him.

I can make him love me. I can.

With every shift of my hips, I focus on his beautiful face and heavy-lidded stare.

He's my everything.

My head rolls from side to side, and Jericho's nostrils flare as he lowers his back to the bed.

"Closer. I need you closer." His palms slide around me, urging me down until I'm flush against his body. His fingers cradle the back of my head until his lips crush against my mouth.

"You're mine, Indy. *Mine.*"

Lifting his hips, he powers into me from below, and each stroke sends me closer to the edge. My fingers curl the sheets as he grips my ass with his other hand, angling my hips so he can go deeper, with the possessiveness I crave.

The words I've been holding back bubble to my lips as my control snaps and my orgasm bears down.

"Jericho—"

He throws his head back and roars my name before I can say *I love you.*

16

FORGE

*I*ndy drifts off to sleep after I clean her up. From the doorway of the bathroom, I stare at the woman in my bed. The one I don't deserve. The one I'll never deserve.

I've never cared about the methods I used to acquire anything in my life. The ends have always justified the means. But this time, I fucking care.

She gave me a gift tonight, and what have I given her in return?

Manipulation. Hidden truths. Enemies.

I fucked up. I thought I could control everything, and I was wrong.

After dressing, I slip out of the bedroom and head to my office. Indy will sleep for hours with the dark curtains blocking the already rising sun, but there's no chance of rest for me. I don't deserve that either. Not until I have answers.

Federov's words haunt me as I shut the door soundlessly and make my way to the desk. Yuri Pallovich's wallet lays open on the wood, mocking me. Telling me I fucked up. I shouldn't have ever allowed Indy to be in danger. That's on me, and I'll never forgive myself for it.

I boot up my laptop and find an email from Federov. The message, sent twelve minutes ago, has only a phone number and three words: *Call me now.*

I don't have my cell phone, because it's lost somewhere in Prague, so I unearth a backup from my desk and punch in Federov's number. Sliding open the floor-to-ceiling glass door in my office, I step outside. The morning sun rises behind me, turning the rippling waves into diamond-topped peaks.

I lift the phone to my ear and connect the call.

Federov answers on the second ring. "We have information."

"Impressive."

"Not impressive. Necessary. My people work fast when my daughter's life is at risk."

I think of how he begged me to get his daughter back on that conference call that seems like it happened years ago. He gave me the name his daughter had been using, and I knew his information was inaccurate because I'd just given India Baptiste a check for a million dollars.

That's when I really started digging into the woman who intrigued me against my will and learned about her sister. I saw my opening. Federov's weakness, which was also quickly becoming my fascination, was ripe to be exploited. I seized the opportunity and brought Indy under my control the most effective way I knew how. I married her.

It was strictly business.

Until it wasn't.

"Tell me everything."

"You will not like it."

"Federov . . ." I say his name on a growl.

"Yuri Pallovich is part of the Bratva that supplies Bastien de Vere with ecstasy, MDMA, and whatever else he's trafficking in that month."

"Are you sure? There's no other connection to anyone else? To you?"

"Not that we can find yet. But I am sure that he will come after you again. De Vere shows no signs of stopping now, and my daughter is in danger because of *you*."

Every word out of Federov's mouth is a jab, which is exactly as he intends. I exploited his weakness, and now he's zeroing in on mine.

"You think I don't know that?" I bite out. "She'll be protected."

"I'm sure that's what you thought before. I will send security to watch over her. Men whose loyalty is absolute."

My molars threaten to crack as my jaw clenches. "She's my wife. I'll take care of her."

"Like you took care of her in Prague? I find her in a fucking veterinarian's office where she was hiding with a bleeding bodyguard who could not protect her!" His voice grows louder and angrier with each reminder of how I failed her. "She was at the mercy of whoever got to her first. What kind of man allows that to happen to his wife?"

An iron fist grips my heart and squeezes. "It won't happen again."

"I do not believe you, Forge. You started this to get the advantage over me. If you have any honor at all, you know what you must do now. This is not about business anymore. This is about keeping my daughter safe from an enemy that targets her only because of you. If you have no honor, I will force your hand."

My teeth grind together. "This conversation is over."

"It is not over until you do the right thing."

I end the call and stare out at the glimmering sea separating Isaac's island from Ibiza. He taught me about honor. Taught me to be a man of my word. What would he have thought of what I've done to India?

Like he was standing beside me, the breeze ruffles my hair.

Do the right thing.

When have I ever cared about that? Or honor?

"I guess we'll see if I have any in me."

*W*aking to a dark room and an empty bed wasn't how I planned to start the day. I dreamed about being wrapped in Jericho's arms, and had hoped to awaken the same way, but his side of the bed is untouched.

Where did he sleep? Did he sleep at all? Is he hurting?

I roll over to check the time on the nightstand clock. Already after noon. No wonder he's not in bed. The fact that he let me sleep in feels so domestic, and a warm, content feeling wraps around me at the kind gesture. Still, I wish he'd woken me so I could take care of him. I have a strong suspicion that the man doesn't know how to slow down, even when he's injured.

After a quick pit stop in the bathroom and another in the closet to find a tank and a pair of shorts, I make a mental note that I need to bring the rest of my clothes here. The meager supplies I have are getting repetitive pretty quickly.

Before, it would have felt wrong to go back to my apartment and box up my things to bring them here, but now . . . that's exactly what I plan to do. This is my home.

I meander out into the hallway, intent on finding my husband, but I spot Dorsey first.

"Good afternoon, Mrs. Forge," she says with a smile, balancing a case of water on her hip. A canvas grocery sack slides off her shoulder. "Is there anything you need?"

"No, but do you need a hand?"

She shifts the bag and readjusts the water as she shakes her head. "No. I'm fine. Just getting a few things for Goliath. He's opted to stay here for his recovery, rather than listening to Mr. Forge and go elsewhere."

"How is Goliath doing? Is he okay?" A rush of guilt washes over me. *I never should have insisted on going to Prague.*

"As grumpy as a lion with a thorn in his paw, but he'll be fine. The doctor was already here to check on him, and said he'll recover just fine. Mr. Forge got a clean bill of health too, and he has the doc on standby should Goliath need anything. He also called Donnigan, Koba, and Bates's families," she says with a sad expression etching lines around her mouth.

This time the guilt doesn't come as a rush, but a stab to the heart. "Oh God. I should've . . . I should've been there. It was my fault."

Dorsey's chin snaps up, and she stares at me in disbelief. "They were doing their jobs, ma'am. They all know the risks they face."

"Still . . ." I wrap my arms around my torso. "I wish I could take it all back."

"Are you looking for Mr. Forge?" Dorsey asks, changing the subject before the tears shimmering in my eyes can fall.

"Yes, if you could point me in his direction, that would be great."

"He's in his office, ma'am."

"Thank you, Dorsey."

She gives me a polite nod, and then disappears into the kitchen. I assume she's heading out through the back of the house to bring Goliath his supplies in his small house that's part of the employee compound at the rear of the island.

I make my way to the office and find the door closed. When I knock, I'm met with silence.

Okay . . . maybe Dorsey was wrong?

I back away to continue my search, but I don't make it two steps before the heavy wooden door swings open behind me with Jericho filling the threshold. I spin around to face him, and he doesn't look like he slept at all. His eyes are bloodshot and his dark hair is a wild mess, like he's been jamming his hands into it over and over.

"Are you okay?" I ask him quietly.

"We need to talk." The grim tone matches Jericho's appearance, and my stomach dips as I follow him into his office. He shuts the door behind me with an ominous click.

"Okay. Whatever you need."

He doesn't look at me until he rounds his desk and sits behind it like he's purposely putting distance between us. But why? Apprehension swirls in my chest.

Jericho pulls a manila folder out of the drawer and slides it across the wood toward me.

"What's that?"

He nods at the folder. "You need to sign it."

"Okay . . . what is it?"

Jericho flips it open and spins it around to face me.

I take two steps closer on unsteady legs and look down at the document.

Petition for Divorce

I BLINK THREE TIMES, but the title of the document doesn't change.

I jerk my head up to stare at him. His haggard

appearance has a completely different meaning than it did only seconds ago. Disbelief tears through me as my hands go clammy and my stomach lurches, sending acid burning up my throat.

"What . . . why . . ."

"Because I want a divorce."

I choke on the sour taste in my mouth as he says the words. *This isn't happening. I'm still dreaming. Right?* I pinch my arm, and the sting tells me I'm wide awake.

"I . . . I don't understand. Why?"

His gaze turns flinty. "I never should have married you to begin with. It was a mistake."

A mistake.

My lower lip wobbles as I try to speak, but no words come out. But Jericho—no, this is *Forge*—doesn't need me to respond. He keeps going.

"I promised you a hundred seventy-five million, but I've doubled it to three fifty. Half will be deposited into your account as soon as you sign. The other half when it's final."

I search the harsh planes and angles of his face for an explanation as to how he could do this *now*, but there's nothing there except his rigid jaw and eyes like the sea at midnight. Fathomless. Bottomless. Completely empty.

"I don't understand. What the hell is really going on here?" I shake my head, like it's going to help me come up with a rational reason. Then one hits me.

The deal with my father. Jericho only needed me as long as it took for him to close the deal.

My stomach twists, and I stumble back. "You signed it, didn't you?"

"Yes. Now you need to sign." Jericho shoves the papers toward the edge of the desk and tosses a pen on top of them.

"You used me, and as soon as you got what you wanted, you're throwing me out." I choke on the words, and my voice is thick with tears. Frozen fingers wrap around my heart and rend it in half. But my devastation has no effect on him.

He stares at me from behind his desk, his hands gripping the arms of his leather chair, like I'm *nothing.* "I told you, I made a mistake. I'm fixing it."

I jab a finger at him. "You're an asshole. A fucking asshole. You get my father to sign the deal, and then you just—"

"What the fuck are you talking about?" he asks, bending forward. "I didn't sign the deal with your father. We haven't done shit with it since before Prague."

Blood roars in my ears as I try to put the pieces together. "Then . . . then why . . ." I look down at the papers in front of me.

He didn't sign the deal, and he still wants me gone. It makes what's happening a hundred times worse.

"We can't be married." His declaration echoes in the room, and there's no mistaking his words.

Searing-hot rage rises from the very depths of my soul.

I snatch the petition off the desk. "So you're just going to shove this at me like I'm nothing? Like *we're* nothing? What the fuck is going on, Jericho?"

He crosses his arms over his chest and leans back in the chair, like I'm not shattering into a million pieces in front of him. "You wanted a divorce. I'm giving you what you want."

I throw the papers at his face. "Well, I don't want it anymore!"

Part of me expects him to rush around the desk and wrap me in his arms and pick me up . . . but he doesn't. *Because he doesn't love me.* Tears burn my eyes as he rises from his seat, plants both palms on the desk, and deals the death blow.

"Too bad, because I do."

I rear back, like he punched me in the gut. I never knew words could cause such intense physical pain, but his shred my damn soul.

One heartbeat. Two heartbeats. Three heartbeats.

"Why?" I whisper the question like it's torn from my dying breath.

"Because this never should've happened to begin with. None of it."

"This was all you!" I scream. My rage takes on a life

of its own as I slam my fist on the desk. "You did this! You manipulated and coerced me into marrying you! And now you just decide you're done? What the fuck, Jericho?"

I heave in a breath and stare at him, but my words have no impact. He's an impenetrable wall.

"Sign the papers, Indy."

Oh no. He did not just fucking use my name like I mean something to him.

"Don't you dare say my name. We *are not friends*!" I shove the chair next to me across the room.

Jericho pushes off the desk and stares down at me. "You're right. We're not. So sign it, and we can both move on with our lives."

Another killing blow. Tears stream down my face and I lash out, wanting him to feel the same pain ripping me apart.

"You draw me in and then push me away, because you can't handle getting close to anyone. All you want is your fucking business and your money and your revenge, and you don't have room for anything else in your goddamned life."

It's like watching a volcano erupt. His expression morphs from stoic to enraged in the space of a heartbeat.

"Did it ever fucking occur to you that I'm doing this to keep you safe? And if it weren't for my fucking revenge, none of this would've ever happened? Bastien would never have come after you! Bates and Donnigan and Koba would be alive, and you wouldn't have been fucking terrorized!"

I stumble back a step. "If you gave a single fuck about me, you wouldn't do this."

His lips flatten into a hard line. "It's over, India. Sign the fucking papers. Take your money and get out."

I stumble back, my body trembling so hard that my teeth chatter. *How could he do this to me? I love him.*

I shove the feeling down. *How could I love someone who could do this to me?*

"Fuck you, Forge." My voice shakes as hard as my hands. "Fuck you. I *hate you*. You want your divorce so fucking bad, to be rid of me?"

I grab sheet after sheet of paper off the desk like a woman possessed, trying to find the one piece that needs my signature. I spot it and grab it, not caring that the paper crumples in my hand. I snatch the pen off the desk and scrawl my signature as the shattered pieces of my heart are ground into dust.

"Here you go. You can fucking have it. And this too."

I rip my ring off my finger and throw it at him. It bounces off his chest and pings when it hits the floor. As I back away, I expect to leave a trail of blood from the destruction he has caused.

But he doesn't seem to care that I'm broken. Jericho watches me with his stony gaze as I reach behind me for the door handle.

Tears blur my vision as I grip the knob.

"You can have your fucking divorce, Forge. But you should know—I didn't want this. I wanted *you*. Only you. *Fuck the money*. I don't want a goddamned thing from you ever again. I can take care of myself. Always have. Always will. So, fuck you."

His mouth opens, but I'm not waiting to hear another goddamned word.

I rip the door open and charge out, slamming it behind me. Blind from the onslaught of tears, I almost collide with Dorsey and her armful of towels.

"Mrs. Forge?"

"Don't call me that ever again," I bite out, swiping at my face. I don't want to cry another tear for him, but I can't stop.

The steward's face goes pale, and as sorry as I should be for taking this out on her, I can't apologize. I'm going to pass out or throw up or both.

"Can I . . . can I help you, Indy?"

Another sob tears free from my lips. "Get me off this fucking island. I'm going home."

*W*ith every step away from the villa, a stupid, naive part of me hopes he'll rush outside, chase me down, and say this was all a huge mistake. That he can't bear the thought of letting me go. That he loves me.

Right. That'll never happen.

Forge doesn't need me. He doesn't need anyone. The glimpse of the man I saw behind the granite wall was a mirage. He doesn't exist.

The memories I have that seem to dispute the fact? *Lies. All lies.* I was dreaming if I thought this could ever work, and I deal in reality. Always have. Always will. Whatever happened here was . . . what did he call it? *A mistake.*

The word hits me like an uppercut to the jaw. I

harden myself against the pain, but the anguish sneaks through.

I won't stay where I'm not wanted. I won't beg for scraps. And I will *never* put myself out like this again.

When I reach the bottom of the stairs, Dorsey is already firing up the engine of the boat, and I don't wait for assistance before I jump on board.

"Pack my stuff up and send it later. Or don't. I don't care," I tell her over the whipping wind. But what I'm really telling myself is *I can live without him.*

And I can. I will. I have no other choice.

I should have known better, and that's the part that kills me the most.

It was a business deal. I wasn't supposed to fall in love with him.

To my surprise, and Dorsey's, Superman and Spiderman also climb aboard.

"What are you doing?" I ask them.

"We're going to watch over you for a while," Spiderman replies, his expression creased with concern. "Just until we're sure that . . ."

I hold up a hand, and he goes quiet.

"I'm not saying this to be a dick, and it's not personal either. All I want is a ride, and after that . . ." I suck in a shaky breath as tears obscure my vision. "I don't want to see anyone connected with Jericho Forge ever again."

All three of them stare at me. The pity in their eyes

stokes the inferno of rage that I'm hoping will meld my broken heart back into something recognizable. *The fires of the forge.*

No. Fuck that. I'll let it stay broken.

"But, ma'am," Superman says, and I shake my head.

"Let's go. Please." I take a seat facing the open water, and stare blindly ahead as they throw off the lines and Dorsey guides the boat away from the dock.

Once we're out to sea and headed back to Ibiza, it's impossible not to take one final look over my shoulder at Isla del Cielo.

I wipe the tears away as I let go of the picture of the future I was able to see for a short time.

It shouldn't hurt so much.

But it does, and I hate him for it.

Forcing myself to turn away, I focus on rebuilding the wall around my heart, brick by brick.

FORGE

*M*y gaze is locked on the boat as it cuts through the water, even though I told myself I wouldn't watch her leave. My fingers uncurl from the fists they've been clenched in, and I press my palm to the glass.

Pain, *physical pain*, sears me.

My mind conjures Indy's face when I told her I wanted her gone. When I *lied to her.* It cuts me, straight to the bone.

I'm a piece of fucking shit. Not worth a goddamn. Uncle Ruben was right.

With a roar, I grab the chair behind my desk and hurl it across the room.

"Fuck!"

It crashes into a painting on the wall and glass shatters. My gaze drops to the signature page of the petition for divorce on the desk. *It's fucking over, and I ended it.*

I spin around and slam my fist into the wall, cracking plaster and busting my knuckles open. Blood drips from my hand, but the pain is nothing compared to the agony tearing me apart inside.

I reach down to pick up her ring, but instead, I drop to my knees.

"*Fuck!*"

Tears, like I haven't cried since the day I lost Isaac, stream down my face.

There's honor for you, Federov. It's fucking hell.

INDIA

I wave off Superman and Spiderman at the entrance to my building. I don't care what their orders are. It doesn't matter to me, because I'll never follow another order given by Jericho Forge.

Each step up to my floor takes a ridiculous amount of effort. It's like I'm walking through wet cement, and it's trying to keep me in place. The whole goddamned building can crumble around me and be washed out to the ocean for all I care.

Why am I so surprised? That's the part that kills me. I set myself up for this, and *I knew better.*

Happily-ever-afters don't start with losing a bet, kidnappings, and negotiations. Only a naive idiot, which I am *not*, would believe otherwise.

But that doesn't mean I can stop the tears or the ache from the gaping hole in my chest.

How could he do this to me?

By the time I reach my door in a sniffling mess, I can barely see where I'm going. I fumble for my keys, which Dorsey retrieved along with my purse from the bedroom, and I unlock my apartment door.

I take two steps inside the silent space, kick the door shut, and collapse against it.

I'm done being strong.

Now I'm just broken.

IT COULD HAVE BEEN minutes or hours or days. I have no idea how much time has passed when the lock above me jiggles as someone pushes a key inside it.

I lift my head, like I've been in a catatonic state, and blink. Afternoon light cuts through the blinds, but the room might as well be pitch black to reflect how I feel.

When the knob turns, I scuttle away from the door, sliding my butt across the tile floor until I ram into the couch.

Who the fuck is coming to my—

The door swings open, and we both scream. Me and Summer.

"What the fuck are you doing here! You scared the hell out of me!" she squeals.

My lungs heave in oxygen and my heart races like I stepped on a live wire. "What the hell are you doing breaking into my apartment?" I ask, my voice coming out in a rasp.

"I have a key! You told me I could stay here whenever I needed."

I blink at her, which apparently is becoming a habit of mine when people say things to me I don't know how to react to. "When did I say that?"

My sister shrugs. *Except . . . she's not really my sister.* The fact hits me like a slap to the face. Shivering, I huddle on the floor as tears flood my eyes again.

"Oh my God, Indy. What's wrong?" Horror flashes across Summer's delicate features, and she drops her bag and slides across the tile to kneel in front of me. "What happened? Who do I need to kill?"

Through my tears, I manage a brittle laugh, but it's muffled as Summer wraps her arms around me.

"You're scaring me, Indy. Please say something."

I snuffle, sounding like the mess I am, and sob into her shoulder. "It's over. My marriage is over."

"Oh shit," she whispers. "Fuck. I'm so sorry, Indy."

And instead of asking me the hundred questions that must be on her mind, Summer squeezes me tighter. Together, we rock on the floor until I have no more tears.

FORGE

"*S*ir, I need to speak with you."

Dorsey's voice comes through my office door after she's knocked three times and I haven't answered.

"Not now," I bite out.

"Sir, with all due respect, I don't care if you don't want to speak to me right now. I need to speak to you."

The door opens, and I grit my teeth. I'm not fit for human interaction right now, and I tried to warn her, but apparently Dorsey is willing to risk her job to say whatever she has on her mind.

"Talk, and then get out."

I don't need to look at her face to see the shock as she surveys my destroyed office. She gapes at the bloody smear on the wall.

My busted knuckles ooze blood and burn every time

I flex my hands, but I deserve more than this pain. Because I'm a piece of shit, and even with all the fucking money in the world, I'll never be worth a damn.

And I never fucking learn.

"Jesus Christ," Dorsey whispers.

"If that's all you have to say, get the fuck out." I hit SEND on an email, because what the fuck else do I have to do but work and get my revenge. That's all I'll ever have.

And I can't even fucking find de Vere. My sources on Ibiza could give me nothing. He's gone to ground, and no one has seen him in days. But I will find him.

The petition for divorce sits on my desk, and I wish I could tear it to shreds. But Indy deserves her freedom, and so I'll give it to her. She'll take the goddamned money too. I don't give a fuck if she wants it or not.

"Your hand, sir. Let me get the first aid kit."

"No."

Dorsey takes another hesitant step forward, like I'm a wounded beast instead of a man.

But maybe she's right. I'm not a fucking man. I don't even merit the description. I couldn't protect my woman when I needed to. I left her at the mercy of anyone. *Her father had to come protect her.*

"I take it . . . Mrs. Forge isn't coming back?"

I grunt in response.

"She asked if I could . . ." Dorsey pauses, probably to stare at the rest of the destroyed room.

"What?" I bark out, clenching my busted hands into fists.

"If I could pack up her things and return them to her."

Another agonizing stab of pain jams into me. "Do it. Do it right now. Get it all out of here."

"Yes, sir." Dorsey takes a few steps backward, as if afraid to let me out of her sight as she leaves. Like I might take a swipe at her. "Is there anything you need before I go, Mr. Forge?"

I finally lift my gaze to the shattered bottles of liquor that used to be on the sideboard in my office.

"A bottle of whiskey. The cheapest shit you can find. Tell everyone I'm not to be disturbed."

An expression of pity curves her lips into a frown, but I don't fucking want anyone's pity. I don't want anything but to get so fucking drunk I can't remember my own name.

The apple doesn't fall far from the tree . . .

"Yes, sir. Right away."

She backs out of the doorway, but before she can close it, I bark out, "Wait."

"Yes?"

"Tell her if she tries to return the money, I'll make a bonfire out of it."

"Yes, sir," Dorsey whispers as she shuts the door and leaves me to wallow in my own fucking misery.

Which is compounded when my phone buzzes. I

don't want to look at it. Don't want to touch it. But I can't help it. It's Federov's number.

I punch the screen to answer. "You don't have to force my hand. I let her go. Now fucking leave me alone."

"Did you now?" Federov sounds surprised.

"What do you want, old man?"

"I thought you would want to know that the Bratva that supplies de Vere's drugs . . . they were not surprised to hear Pallovich took a side job. They also owe me a favor, and I called it in. They're going to set a trap for de Vere. I'm going to help you get your revenge."

My revenge. Feels fucking hollow now.

"Fine. Now leave me the fuck alone."

"No, I wish to talk about the deal—"

I end the call and hurl the phone across the room.

Fuck the deal. Fuck everything.

I don't remember falling asleep, or climbing up on the couch, or being covered with a blanket. But when I open my eyes, that's exactly where I am. A steaming cup of tea sits on the table in front of me, and before I see her, I know Alanna is here.

Summer called her because she's never seen me like this. I've never broken down like I thought my life was over before. Not even the day when I realized our mom—who wasn't actually my mom—was never coming back for us.

How I am I ever going to tell Summer the truth? That she's not my sister? That her mom was my father's mistress and kidnapped me?

My stomach twists and flips. I want to burrow my head under the blanket and forget about all of it, but Alanna peeks around the couch and sees my eyes open before I can feign sleep and avoid the conversation that is inevitably coming next.

"Oh, honey. I'm so sorry." Her lips quiver as she comes around to sit beside me and throws both arms around my neck. "So, so sorry," she whispers.

I swallow the lump in my throat and try to speak, but the words get caught.

"Here, drink this." She presses a mug of hot tea into my shaky hands.

Dutifully, I sip the chamomile-flavored water. If nothing else, Alanna believes in the restorative powers of a cup of tea like she'd been born in Britain rather than America.

"You don't need to be sorry," I say, handing the mug back to her. With how much I'm trembling, I don't trust myself not to spill it everywhere. "You didn't do this. I did it to myself."

"I refuse to believe that whatever happened is all because of you. It takes two to tango, my dear."

It's a phrase she often pulled out for Summer when she was going through one tumultuous breakup after another. But I'm not my sister, whose heart bounces back instead of shattering.

She's not my sister, I remind myself, and another tear trails down my cheek.

"Indy, sweetheart, talk to me. Please. You're scaring an old woman, and you know that's not fun."

I look around the room for my sis—Summer—but she's gone. "Where is she?"

"Summer had to go back to work. She came home on her lunch hour because she didn't want to use the work facilities to . . . you know . . ."

I would have sworn it was impossible to bring a smile to my face at that moment, but the reminder that my sister can't take a crap in a public restroom manages to do it.

"My flat is now her designated toilet? Wait, no, she said she's been staying here." The smile fades when I remember she works for Juliette Preston Priest.

Alanna nods. "She told me you said it was okay."

Another Summer white lie. "I didn't, but I would've. It's not a big deal. How is her job going?"

I hate that I feel petty when I ask, because it reminds me of how Juliette was so shocked that Forge had "settled down." I still remember what he said in reply. *"Because I hadn't met Indy yet."*

Bullshit. Shivers ripple through me, and the tears slide down my face. Alanna reaches out to wipe them away before I squeeze my eyes shut.

"Why don't we talk about you first, dear?"

I shake my head. "I would prefer not to."

"I know, but sometimes you have to get it out before you can start healing."

Healing? That sounds like a foreign concept if I've

ever heard one. I plan to harden, since the chances of me healing are slim to none.

I can't bring myself to talk about what happened with Forge, so I blurt, "Summer isn't my sister."

Alanna's eyes go wide and her mouth drops open. "What? What are you talking about?"

I bite down on my lip, wishing I hadn't said anything. The last thing I want to do is cause anyone else even a fraction of the pain that I'm feeling right now.

"I met my father," I say, pausing when I remember that Alanna doesn't know anything about this. I didn't tell her *anything* because not only am I a shitty daughter, I'm also a shitty adopted daughter.

"Your father? How? When?" She curls her hands into the blanket that covers me.

I inhale a shaky breath and let it all spill out. How I was kidnapped. Why Summer was kidnapped. How my father found me. Why Forge married me. Why Bastien was causing trouble. Through it all, Alanna sits on the couch, staring at me in disbelief.

"Oh, my goodness gracious. If this is what you've been holding in, no wonder you're a mess, sweetheart." She pulls me into another hug and squeezes me almost hard enough to break a rib.

My tears, which I thought were dried up, pour out like a tidal wave.

"Shh . . . shh . . . it's okay. It's all going to be okay,"

she murmurs, soothing me in a way that I never let her as a prickly and wary teenager.

"How can it ever be okay? My sister isn't my sister!" My voice breaks on the last word, and I meet Alanna's gaze. She reaches out to smooth my wild hair away from my face before her expression turns authoritative.

"Don't you ever say that about Summer. I don't give a damn if there's not a single drop of blood shared between you, because that's not what matters. I may not have carried you in my womb, or given birth to either of you, but you're my daughters all the same. Family doesn't just mean blood, Indy. Family is much more than that."

"But—"

She shakes her head. "No buts. You raised Summer from the day she was born. You protected her. Fed her. Clothed her. Love her more than life itself. Does that mean nothing to you?"

A tear in my soul mends together at her words.

"It means *everything*," I whisper.

Alanna's lips pinch together. "Damn right it does, and don't you ever forget that. Summer will always be your sister."

I lean against her shoulder, soaking up her comforting presence as I let her words sink in and wrap around me.

Summer will always be my sister. No matter what.

"You're right. I just . . ." I look past her to the closed shades, trying to find the words I want to say.

She squeezes my knee. "You've been hit with the equivalent of a dump-truck load of information and no time to process it. At least, that's how it looks from where I'm sitting."

"Yeah. Something like that," I say, dragging my gaze back to hers.

"What about Mr. Forge?" she asks, her tone hesitant.

I bite down on my lip as my vision turns blurry. "I don't want to talk about it. Not yet."

Alanna pats my knee. "Then you won't talk about it yet. But we do need to talk about the man in a suit at the door of your building who's acting like a bulldog and checking the ID of everyone who enters. And then there's the one who watches from a black sedan in the same place they parked before."

Spiderman and Superman.

I swipe at my tears. "They need to leave."

Her gaze locks on mine. "Are you in danger, Indy? Is there more going on that we need to know about?"

I can't help but picture Bates and Donnigan's bodies in the hallway of the hotel in Prague, and I utter a silent prayer for them. "I don't know anymore. I don't know anything at all anymore."

FORGE

I toss the rest of my shit in the duffel, zip it up, and throw it over my shoulder as I leave the bedroom. There's no reason for me to stay.

Dorsey waits in the hallway, another duffel in hand. One that I don't want to look at or acknowledge.

Inside, I've iced over like the Chesapeake used to do in the winters of my childhood. It's better to feel nothing.

The hole in my chest might still gape, but I'm pretending it's not there.

"You're in charge of the island."

"Yes, sir. When will you be back?"

I shrug because I don't have an answer for her.

Maybe never.

Isla del Cielo was never meant to be a lifeless, soulless, loveless place. But that's exactly what I've made it. Isaac wouldn't be proud. Not even a little fucking bit.

"Take care, Dorsey."

I stalk out of the house and head for the chopper.

"*S*he has to talk to us eventually."

Summer's voice travels all the way to my bedroom because she's never known how to whisper. I've always called it her whisper-yell instead.

"She will when she's ready, dear. Just give her time."

Pots clang, and the scent of garlic wafts down the hall. *Alanna's cooking.*

"Should I quit my job?" Summer asks. "I feel like I should because Forge got it for me. I'm essentially working for the enemy, aren't I?"

"Keep going like you have been. Get as much out of it as possible, and then you can decide."

With a groan, I roll facedown on the soft sheets of my bed. I've lost track of the days. Alanna has hovered over me like I'm a terminal patient, instead of just brokenhearted because I was stupid enough to fall in love with the wrong man.

Love is for idiots. That's the only thing I know for sure now.

I trudge to the bathroom, and the vision in the mirror is terrifying enough to scare the boogeyman. My hair is a rat's nest, and my eyes are puffy and bloodshot like I've gone on a three-day bender.

My mouth tastes like a litter box. I reach for my toothbrush, because at least that's one problem I can fix. I try to smooth out my hair the best I can, but it's a lost cause, and there's nothing I can do about my face.

I square my shoulders and walk into the living room like I didn't just wake up as an extra in *Night of the Living Dead.*

Obviously, Alanna and Summer heard sounds of life from the bathroom, because they're both standing and facing the hallway when I walk into the open kitchen and living area of my flat.

Alanna has moved into the guest room, and Summer has stopped by often, judging from how many times I've heard her voice. Or maybe I dreamed that. Who knows.

"How are you feeling, dear?" Alanna asks like I'm ill, instead of throwing the world's most intense pity party.

"I'm fine." I shove a hand into my hair, and my fingers get stuck.

"You look like hell," Summer says as I tug them free.

"Thanks. I appreciate that."

She shakes her head, sending her blond waves, that no longer look like mine, flying. "That's not what I meant. I mean you look like you've been through hell. I'm still so sorry, Indy. I wish . . . I wish I could fix this for you like you've always fixed everything for me."

Immediately, my mind rewinds to the memory of that time I married a guy to save Summer from being sold to sex slavers. *Nope, still not distant enough.*

"It's fine. I'm fine. I'll be fine." I give her a lame thumbs-up.

Summer's eyebrows wing up to her hairline. "That's a lot of fine for someone who—"

"Enough, Summer. Indy, do you want some tea? Sandwich? Soup? I've made a little bit of everything. You've barely eaten in days, and you need to."

For the first time since I came back to my apartment, my stomach rumbles with hunger. I guess that's a good sign.

"Whatever you've made is good. I'm not picky."

Alanna bustles into the kitchen and busies herself putting together a plate for me.

"Want to sit outside? It's nice," Summer says.

I glance out the window and realize the sun is setting. "What day is it?"

"Friday."

I've lost track of two days. Not as bad as I thought.

"How's the job going?" I ask, remembering what she said about feeling like she was working for the enemy.

If that Juliette bitch was mean to Summer, I'll tell her where to get off. *Because that's what sisters do.* Alanna was right; there's nothing in this world that would make Summer anything other than my sister. *Family is more than blood.*

Forge knew that too. He had Isaac . . . until Bastien killed him.

My heart clenches again, but I push away the feeling. I refuse to hurt for him, not after he threw me out—for the second time—like I was trash.

Summer's expression goes blank, like she's hiding something from me.

"You can tell me. I promise I'm not going to fall apart again."

"Pretty good."

Her reply has me raising my eyebrows. "Define *pretty good.*"

"It's not bad. I mostly run and fetch like a gofer, but I've gotten to learn a lot. I've made some really great contacts." Her shoulders slump. "I won't keep working for her, though. I'm going to put in my notice."

I shake my head, proud that I have zero inclination to cry. "No, don't. There's no reason to quit. I'm not worried about it. Make sure it's worth putting on your résumé."

"But—"

When Summer tries to object, I cut her off.

"What happened between me and Forge had nothing to do with your boss."

"What did it have to do with then? You're killing me here. I need to know if I should be hunting him down to kill him, or if he gets to live."

My fierce, loyal sister.

"It ran its course. That's all."

Summer surveys my puffy eyes and gives me a *that's bullshit and you know it* look.

"I caught feelings, and he didn't." I say it in a way that Summer will understand. She's always been of the *catch flights, not feelings* mentality, at least when she's coming off a breakup.

"Oh . . . shit. I'm sorry. That's . . . not cool."

And it's as humiliating as I imagined.

"I just need some time to get it out of my system and move on."

"Is that why . . ." Summer presses her lips together instead of finishing her sentence.

"Is that why what?" I ask.

"Juliette's been asking about you a lot. And then she said something about you and Bastien—"

I reach out and wrap my palm around Summer's wrist. "Stay away from Bastien. Far away. You hear me?

Actually, you need to go buy a taser, and if you ever see him again, shock the fuck out of his ass before he can get close to you."

Her stunned gaze drops to where I'm gripping her wrist. "Whoa. Why?"

"He's no good. He's deep in the drug scene, way deeper than I ever realized. And dangerous as hell. Don't go anywhere near him. *Ever.*"

Summer bobs her head, and I think I've gotten through to my sister with a warning on the first try.

Just to make sure she understands, I add, "He's the one who ordered those kids to trash Alanna's efficiency apartment."

From the kitchen, Alanna gasps. "He did *not.*"

"He did that, and who knows what else. We all need to be very careful. Don't take unnecessary risks. Use your common sense. I don't want anything happening to either of you. I couldn't bear it."

After we finish eating, Summer asks me if I want to come out with her to a club tonight. "The best way to get over someone is to get under someone else."

"I don't think so." I give her a hug and tell Alanna, "You don't have to stay here. I'll be okay. I'm just going to lick my wounds for a while, and I'll join the living again. Just not yet."

With concerned expressions, they both study me.

"I'll be back to normal soon. Just . . . give me a little space."

INDIA

*T*wo weeks later, Summer has had enough of my hibernating. Apparently, she doesn't buy that I'm too busy with my latest Netflix series binge to leave the flat.

"You have to get out of here before you become furniture. Seriously, Indy. This isn't you. You need to be out doing things. Living. That's what you love."

Love. What bullshit.

But I'm not about to spew my jaded views at my sister right now. "I showered today. What more do you want from me?"

Summer's temper snaps. "I want you to leave this fucking flat and stop scaring Alanna to death! This isn't only affecting you, you know."

And here comes the guilt. "Fuck. I'm sorry. I . . . didn't think about that."

"Probably because you're only feeling sorry for yourself." She plops down on the table between me and the TV. "So what if your marriage is over. Your life isn't. Go out and fucking live it. Your phone won't stop buzzing with invites to games all over the world. People are talking about Prague and what a beast you were. If you don't capitalize on it now, you might never get another chance like this."

"Wait." I hold up a finger. "How did you get in my phone?"

"You used my birthday as a pass code. It wasn't hard."

It reminds me of when Forge hacked into my phone, and now I know it wasn't for the reason he gave me. He already knew my sister had been kidnapped.

I slam down the lid on the iron box that I'm keeping all Forge thoughts in. *Stop thinking about him. It's over. He tossed you out like rotten fish. Focus on the present.*

I have my winnings from the Prague Grand Prix, and I have a $5 million side bet to collect from Belevich to add to my stash. And apparently, I have invitations to play all over the world.

The old Indy would scan through them with glee in her eyes, but I feel no such excitement. I feel . . . nothing. Like I'm dead inside.

Stop being so dramatic. That's Summer's MO.

But I've also never fallen in love like this before . . . *Slam. The. Lid. Down.*

I glance at my sister's concerned face. Someday, I have to tell her that her mother was a kidnapper who lied about me being dead to my father, but not today.

"Where's my phone?"

My sister hops off the table and scampers into the kitchen with way too much energy. A moment later, she drops it in my lap. I tap in the code, and sure enough, she's opened all the texts that have been sent for the last couple weeks. Many of the games have already taken place.

I get to Belevich's message.

BELEVICH: *I'm back on Ibiza. I've got your money.*

I WANT the money because I earned it fairly, and I'd like to thank him for what he did for me in Prague.

When grief rises up to swamp me, I can't lock it down in the box. I should have gone to the funerals. Should have apologized to the families of the men who died. Told them it was my fault. But I've been hiding in my apartment like a little coward.

That stops today. I'm done hiding from the world. I've never needed a man in my life to define me before, and I don't need one now.

I almost believe my own pep talk. At least that's progress.

I respond to Belevich.

INDY: Address?

HIS REPLY IS ALMOST INSTANTANEOUS.

I look up at my sister, finally feeling like I have a purpose. "I need to go out."

Summer's smile could light the world with its brilliance. "Good. That's exactly what I wanted to hear. Plus, I'm sure the security guys who have been trading shifts outside the building for the last couple weeks will like a change of scenery."

"Still? They didn't go away?"

Summer's blond hair swings from side to side. "Not except to trade off shifts with some guys I didn't recognize."

My first thought is to call Forge and ask him who else he sent, but I won't. *Ever.*

Instead, I call Alanna, tell her I'm ready to rejoin the land of the living, and go back to my room to change into clothes that haven't been worn for three days straight.

Time to find Belevich.

I HIT the steps to my building where Superman is standing guard.

Why would Forge still have them watching out for me?

I want to read into it. Tell myself that Forge still cares, but I can't lie to myself like that. *He's doing it because of the guilt. That's all.* Even though pain stabs into my heart, I tell myself I feel nothing. *Absolutely nothing.* Numbness is a hell of a lot easier to deal with than the feelings that I still can't manage to stamp out, no matter how hard I try.

Superman straightens as I walk by. "Ms. Baptiste. Are you going somewhere? Do you need a ride?"

The sound of my name on his lips, the one I've had for almost my entire life, nearly sends me running back into the building. I don't know if the divorce could be final this fast, but clearly, Forge's people know our marriage is definitely over.

"Yes and no," I tell him. I jog to the sidewalk, intent on heading out to the main road so I can hail a taxi, because owning a car here has never made sense.

He follows on my heels. "We can give you a ride. That's what we're here for."

"No, thank you. I'm going to get a cab."

"Ma'am, if you'd please let us drive you—"

I pause and spin around to stare at him through his Clark Kent glasses. "I know you're following orders, but I'm not your problem anymore. Go home. I'm sure you have a million better things to do."

To myself, I add, *instead of being here and giving me some hope that there's a way out of my nightmare.*

"But we can't—"

I wave and keep walking.

Maybe it's stupid to turn down security after everything that has happened, but I refuse to lean on them for safety. I have to fend for myself. That's the way it's always been and always will be.

Yet, a black car follows my taxi all the way to the address Belevich texted me. When we arrive at the gated entrance to the villa, I pay and hop out of the back.

There's a keypad to the right, and I press the intercom button. Instead of someone asking me to identify myself, the gates swing open.

Here I go.

My phone buzzes with another message, and I ignore it.

It's hot as hell in the engine room of the cargo ship *Fortuna*, but that's where I belong. I'm covered in grease and sweat, having given the engineer whose job it was to replace this gasket a break so I could punish myself some more.

I've worked myself into the ground, barely sleeping. Eating just enough to keep my energy going. Drinking like a fish as soon as I hit my cabin, and praying I won't dream about her again.

But prayers from a guy like me don't get answered that often, which means I'm cursed to dream about her every fucking night. I can still smell her scent on my clothes. Can still hear her voice in my head.

I did the honorable thing. The noble thing. And being noble fucking blows.

I've heard from Federov once more. His Bratva connections have a buy set with Bastien for two days from now. After I landed on the *Fortuna,* I called up more security and ordered them to keep an eye on Indy 24/7, but not to give me any reports.

But still, the reports came in whether I wanted them or not.

I lower the wrench and grab a grease rag out of the pocket of my pants to wipe off my face and hands. My phone buzzes again, and I fish it out because I have a feeling it's not going to stop.

SMITH: She's at Belevich's. We can't get inside. Unless you want us to ram the gate.

FUCK. There's no question who the *she* is, and even just seeing the fucking pronoun makes my gut knot. I can still see her face when I told her we were done. I'll never get that image out of my head. I'll never forgive myself for it either. For any of it.

SMITH: What do you want us to do? Try to get inside? This is the first time she's left her flat.

. . .

IT'S a shitty reminder of what I did. I can't imagine the vibrant, incredible woman I knew holing up in her apartment for weeks. *I hurt her . . . no, I fucking devastated her.*

There's no way she could have possibly been in lo—

I can't even manage to think the whole word because it's so fucking ridiculous. Indy didn't care about me like that. How could she? I lied, manipulated, coerced, and generally bullied her.

But that didn't stop me from falling in love with her.

I type out a response to the text with fingers that smudge my screen with the remaining grease.

FORGE: Watch from where you are. If there's any sign of distress, drive through the gate.

AFTER WHAT FEDEROV had told me—that Belevich is the one who helped Indy get out of the hotel and got Goliath help for his gunshot wound—I'm not worried about Belevich hurting her.

SMITH: Yes, sir. Will do.

FORGE: Keep me posted.

I SHOVE my phone back into the pocket of the coveralls I haven't worn since the last time I punished myself at sea in the months after Isaac died, and throw myself back into work.

*B*elevich opens the glass door of his villa before I hit the stamped concrete stairs leading to it.

"Here I thought I'd get to keep my money because you didn't want it."

"I never said that."

He surveys me, and I feel like he sees too much—my sharpened features, eyes that may never not be puffy again, and clothes that hang a little too loose on my frame due to missing so many meals.

"You look like you've been gambling for a week with no sleep."

"Nope, just going through a divorce."

His eyebrows shoot upward. "That's something I didn't expect to hear." He tilts his head to one side. "When did that happen?"

"After Prague. It's not important. I'll take the money and get out of your way."

His expression guarded, he steps back into the white stucco villa. "That's not the Russian way. Come, I will teach you. If you want your cash, you will drink with me."

I release an annoyed sigh and follow him inside. I'm not about to walk away without my five million this time.

Belevich's villa is a wide-open floor plan with white stucco walls and red accents. He leads me across the tile floor out to the pool that's in the center courtyard. He snaps out an order in Russian, and a woman in white slacks and a white blouse hurries off.

"If you would prefer the ocean view—"

"No," I say, cutting him off. "This is fine. I don't need to see anything but my money."

He gestures to a seat at an ornate metal table. "So, who ended it? You, I presume."

I grip the sun-warmed arms of the chair and pause in the act of lowering myself into it. "Drop it, or I leave."

"You would leave five million dollars behind just because you don't want to talk about it . . . Hmmm . . . I think my guess was wrong then. He ended it, and you were not ready to say good-bye." Belevich sits across from me, smoothing his goatee with his thumb and forefinger. "I wonder why he would do such a thing. Then again, Forge is unpredictable."

I push up from the chair, about to make my point and leave, but he waves me down as the woman returns with a bottle of vodka and two shot glasses. *Not shocking.* Then again, I'm not going to turn it down if he's going to keep probing about Forge. Maybe it'll help numb the pain.

"One drink, and I'm gone."

"You could use more than one. You look like shit."

With a fake smile pasted on my face, I bare my teeth at him. "We already covered this ground."

"Just being honest."

I glance up at him as he splashes booze into the glasses. "Don't worry about trying to be charming or anything. I'm not in the market for ex-husband number two, and never will be."

"Ah . . . Bitterness is hard to overcome."

"Save it."

He hands a glass to me, and instead of waiting for whatever he has to say next, I toss it back, relishing the smooth, cool flavor of the liquor.

"You need teaching. You didn't even wait for me to make a toast."

I hold my glass out to him. "I might be Russian by blood, but it's not like I got an instruction manual."

He pours me another shot and lifts his own. "I'm surprised your father did not urge you to go to Russia. He would want you protected at all costs." When I shrug, Belevich tilts his head again. "He does not know about the divorce, does he?"

"I haven't told him."

"Not very smart," he says before adding something in Russian that there's no way in hell I can repeat back to him. Instead, I tap the rim of my glass against his and shoot the vodka.

"If your father knew you were without protection, he would have many things to say about it. I'm surprised Forge did not tell him so he could send his people to look after you. If you need help finding security, I know a reputable agency. Given what happened in Prague, I do not think it's safe—"

I silence him with a raised hand. "Security is out front in a black sedan, blocked by your gates. I've got a babysitter from Forge whether I want one or not."

"Then why . . ." Belevich's eyes narrow. "I do not understand what Forge is thinking then."

"I don't have any answers for you, and I don't care." The second part is a lie, and we both know it.

Belevich leans back in his chair, balancing on two legs like he did in the vet's office. "I would have sworn . . ."

"What?"

He purses his lips, and I consider pouring myself another shot as I wait for him to speak. "I would've sworn Forge had feelings for you. In Prague, he did not act like a man who wanted to divorce his wife."

The ache in my jaw intensifies with every grind of my teeth. I'll be lucky to have any left at this rate. There's no avoiding this conversation. No matter what I do, Belevich isn't going to drop it, and I want my money.

"I don't know. Your guess is as good as mine. He blindsided me the day after we got home."

Belevich rubs his thumb over his lip. "Interesting . . ."

"To you, maybe." I reach for the bottle, but he snatches it off the table before my fingers touch the glass.

"Don't you think the timing is suspect? You were in danger, he was in danger, your father was there, and then you come home . . . and it's over?"

"What's your point?"

Belevich settles his chair back on four legs and pours himself another shot of vodka, neglecting to fill mine. *Asshole.* "Did your father speak to Forge?"

"Of course."

"What did he say?"

"I don't know. I wasn't there."

Belevich lifts the glass to his lips and sips. "Don't you want to know what he said?"

I look up to the clouds that float by overhead and then back to the man across from me. "Should I?"

"I would, if I were you. Maybe ask your father what

he said to your husband to make him divorce you after he was falling in love with you."

My fingers clench around the empty shot glass. "Don't say that. Forge wasn't—"

"Bullshit. I watched him with you in Prague. That was not an indifferent man. That was a proud man. A man who knew what he had."

"And then he threw it all away like I was nothing," I add, my voice dropping to a low rasp.

"Which makes no sense to me." He drums the fingers of one hand on the edge of the metal table. "If I were you, I would be asking your father what he did. That is the key." He shoves back his chair and rises. "Now, I am done with relationship advice for the day. I will get you your money."

Ten minutes later, I lean down to the open window of the black sedan in front of Belevich's house, a heavy duffel bag weighing down my right side.

"I need a ride. I'm not taking a taxi home."

*S*uperman and Spiderman make small talk all the way home, but I'm lost in my thoughts. *Was Forge really falling in love with me? Could that even be possible?*

Because goddammit, if he was, what the hell did my father say to make him push me away?

Belevich was right. Russian daddy dearest and I need to have a little discussion, because spending the last couple weeks curled up under my covers, or on my couch and unshowered, is *not* typical India Baptiste behavior. That was brokenhearted Indy behavior, and that shit ends *now*.

My mission is clear—figure out if my father torpedoed my relationship.

But what if Belevich is wrong? I don't want to believe he could be. I saw how Jericho looked at me. He didn't go above and beyond in Prague because I was just a means to an end. There was nothing in that for him. It was all about me. *He* was all about me.

As for his revenge with Bastien putting me in danger? *Screw that.* I'm not going to let that motherfucker take this from me too.

Watch out, world. I'm back.

Before I make it all the way home, I text Belevich.

INDY: What is Federov's number?

I COULDN'T TYPE *FATHER*. It didn't feel right. Probably because it doesn't feel like he really is. His story is crazy enough that no one could have made it up. Truth is always stranger than fiction. Plus, Russian oligarchs have more important things to do than spin stories about a missing daughter like she's the long-lost princess Anastasia.

Regardless, having a father doesn't change who I am as a person. How the hell did I forget that I'm street-smart, confident, and resourceful? When did I decide to take life lying down? That's not me. A little time getting used to the way the other half lives, and realizing I'm not an orphan, isn't going to change me.

No one is holding my sister hostage, and I'm not

afraid anymore. I want answers, and I'm going to get them.

We park in front of my building, and I open the door and shoulder the bag. "Thanks for the ride, boys. I'm going to need one later."

Both men turn around and look at me like I've undergone a personality transplant. *Nope*, I just remembered who the hell I am.

Superman hops out of the car. "I'll escort you up to your flat, Ms. Baptiste."

"It's Indy, and that's not necessary. Do you two have an end date for your babysitting? Because my schedule's about to get busy."

They look at each other, and a silent conversation passes between them while I unstick my legs from the leather seat.

"Not at present, ma'am—Indy."

"Good," I say with my first genuine smile in weeks. "Pack your bags, and I hope you don't mind flying commercial. I don't have private-jet money just yet."

They gape at me as I climb out of the back seat and high step it up to my building.

The sun is shining, I've got hard-earned cash in my bag, and I'm ready to prepare for phase two—find my father and get an explanation about what the hell happened between him and Forge.

And then I've got a few things to say to my soon-to-be ex-husband. I'm not letting the Kraken go so easily.

INDIA

The soaring frescoed ceilings, marble columns, and gold-and-cream interior of the Casino de Monte Carlo is just as awe inspiring and palatial as the last time I stepped foot through these doors. I scan the sumptuous gaming floor, but there are no security guards heading my way to throw me out. *Bonus.*

A casual glance over my shoulder reassures me that Superman and Spiderman are tailing me with just enough distance not to be obviously noticeable. Then again, at a place like this, private security is as common as poker chips, so it's not like they'll attract much attention. If anything, they'll probably add to my cachet.

Have they told Jericho I'm here? The question has been plaguing me since our flight out of Ibiza. Along with . . . *Would he come here to find me if he knew?* I'm not sure I'm ready for an answer to that one, though.

I push both questions out of my mind as best I can and focus on tonight. First up, a meeting on neutral ground, and then in an hour, a high-stakes game Summer reminded me I was invited to. My fingers flex as if anxious for the slide of the cards between them.

Play the man, not the game. I'm ready.

Earlier in my suite, I changed into a jade-green dress with a keyhole neckline and my Alexander McQueen peep-toe pumps, curled my hair into big beachy waves, and applied my makeup with a ruthless hand. If eyeshadow were a weapon of war, I'd be assured victory. Finally, I pulled out the big guns—my Alexander McQueen skull purse that looks like you're wearing brass knuckles when you carry it.

Walking through the casino, I finally feel like my old self again. Actually, *better* than my old self, because I have a different kind of confidence wrapped around me. It's not the brittle confidence-by-necessity I used to have. It's something deeper, more innate. *I have a purpose, and it goes far deeper than winning a simple poker game.*

On the way to the bar, I catch a flash of auburn hair swinging over a shoulder as someone does a double take.

"No. Impossible. *She is not here.*"

The haughty British accent stops me in midstride. My instincts tell me to keep walking, but I can't ignore that voice. Slowly, I turn to face Poppy de Vere . . . and Juliette Preston Priest.

Really? I send a glance toward the masterpiece of a ceiling, asking the man upstairs why he couldn't leave Jericho's former mistress out of this. I get no response.

Poppy's perfectly applied nude lip curls as her brown gaze drags from my hair to my heels. I grip my newfound confidence even tighter as Superman and Spiderman retreat to a respectful distance.

"Poppy. Juliette." I say their names politely. "What an interesting coincidence. I didn't expect to see you here either. Especially together." I bite my tongue before I can say anything else, if for no other reason than to save Summer's job.

"What are *you* doing here?" Juliette asks in a haughty tone. "Trying to drum up your next rich ex-husband? I hear it's a lot harder to do the second time around."

"Excuse me?" I ask, holding my head high. These two women are insignificant, but still, they've clearly heard the news and have no qualms about stabbing at fresh wounds.

"I told you Jericho would never settle down. It wasn't at all surprising to hear he filed for divorce."

I keep my smile fixed in place even as her swipe threatens to shatter my composure. A small part of me has been holding out hope that he wouldn't actually file the papers I signed, but I'll never admit that to them.

"You know everything, don't you, Juliette? Except how to hang on to a man yourself, it seems."

Her features turn hawkish. "I wouldn't be too smug if I were you. It won't take him long to replace you. It never does after they go slumming for kicks."

My teeth grind together, and only my best poker face can stop me from baring them at her.

Poppy saves me from having to reply. "I'm surprised you're not sniffing after my brother again."

My gaze cuts to the sharply contoured lines of her face. "Have you seen your brother lately? Or is he too busy kidnapping people and slinging drugs?"

Poppy's face drains of color before she bolts forward. "*How dare you!*"

I sense Superman and Spiderman moving toward us, but I hold up a hand over my shoulder.

"I dare because it's the truth. If you want to see him again, you should probably find him soon. I doubt he'll be breathing much longer."

Poppy's face doesn't look nearly as elegant when it's contorted in rage. "You're lying. My brother would *never*."

"Might want to ask him a few questions, Poppy." I flick open my clutch to peek at my phone for the time. "And now I'm late for my meeting. If you'll excuse me."

"You don't know anything, you little—"

A gruff Russian-accented voice comes from behind

me. "I doubt very much that you want to finish your sentence, madam."

Ah. My father found me before I found him.

I turn to look at him, this time dressed in an elegant tuxedo, starched white shirt, and diamond studs. "Good evening. I apologize for running late."

Juliette Preston Priest stares open-mouthed between me and my father. *Does she know who he is?* Or maybe she's thinking that I've got daddy issues, which I undoubtedly do, but not like that.

"It is no problem. If you will excuse us, ladies." His emphasis on the word *ladies* indicates he thinks they're nothing of the sort, which I find endlessly amusing. "My daughter and I have much to discuss."

Juliette's mouth snaps shut and Poppy stares at her, clearly uncertain what is going on. I wink at them and turn to strut away as they hurl invisible daggers at my back.

"Ms. Baptiste," Superman says, moving closer to my side.

"It's fine. We'll be at the bar. I'm perfectly safe."

"Yes, ma'am. We'll be close, though."

My father holds out an arm. "After you."

I lead the way to the bar, walking past the already crowded craps tables and the clicking roulette wheel as people hold their breath, waiting to see where the ball will land. When we stop in front of the antique wooden bar, my father signals to the bartender, and the service is immediate and efficient.

"Two Kauffmans," he orders.

"Club soda with lime for me," I say, because I'm not drinking vodka tonight.

He looks over at me, his steel-gray brows raised. "Ah, you do not drink when you play. That must be one of Queen Midas's secrets."

"It's not much of a secret."

Moments later, the bartender slides three drinks in front of us.

Federov wraps a massive paw around the delicate crystal of one and raises it. "To your victory tonight."

"I'll drink to that." I lift my glass and tap the rim against his.

My father tips the vodka back as I sip the bubbly water. When he lowers his empty glass to the antique wooden bar, his blue eyes seem to catalog every aspect of my appearance. He told me I was the very image of my mother and confirmed it by showing me her picture, and I wonder if he's thinking of her now. But if he is, he doesn't speak of it.

With a glance toward the direction we came from, he asks, "Do you want to tell me what that was about on the floor? The brassy one looked like she wanted your head, and the other did not seem any friendlier."

"It was nothing. They're nothing."

He lifts his chin. "Compared to you, I agree. But still, if there are threats to be aware of, I wish to know."

I point over my shoulder at Spiderman and Superman. "As you can see, I still have protection against threats."

"I noticed. But even then, you can never be too careful. I only just found you again, Illyana. I will not lose you now."

"Indy. My name is Indy."

His lips compress together as if he wants to contradict me, but he doesn't. "Indy. You will have to be patient with me."

With small talk out of the way, I get down to the reason I called and asked him to meet with me. "What did you say to my husband?"

"What do you mean?" His tone is curious, but he has to know to what I'm referring.

"Everything was fine until we got home, and then suddenly it wasn't. If you said something to him, I need you to tell me what. Because there's no way in hell he should've been sliding a petition for divorce across the desk to me after Prague. Something happened, and I want to know what."

He narrows his eyes. "Why must it be me who said something? Forge is his own man. He doesn't bow to anyone's dictates. Not even mine."

"You're mixing enough bullshit into the truth that I can smell it from here. Forge was falling in love with me. You know it. I know it. But you said *something*, and I want to know what it was." I swirl my club soda and flick at the napkin beneath it with my thumb.

Instead of answering my question, he tosses back the second shot of vodka with the ease of lifelong practice. "Do you really want the man back after he spurned you?"

"That's my decision, and I need to know what kind of meddling I'm dealing with so I can make it."

His barrel-shaped chest rises and falls as deep bellows of laughter ring out from his lips. When he finally calms himself, he uses a cocktail napkin to wipe tears from his eyes. I slide off my stool, my gaze boring into him, because I am not amused.

"You are my daughter. There is no doubt about that." The mirth fades from his face. "But whatever was said between me and Forge is just that—between me and Forge. A conversation between men is not one to be shared."

I release a harsh breath and glance up at the crystal chandelier above us, seeking patience or divine guidance to save me from this patriarchal bullshit.

"How about I make you a deal then?"

His head tilts to the side in a move I have to believe is very Russian. "What kind of deal?"

I flick open my clutch and check the time. "How good are you at pulling strings?"

"Excellent," my father replies, and something glints in his gaze.

"Then tonight is our first father-daughter poker game. When I beat you, you're going to tell me exactly what was said in your *conversation between men*, and you're not going to leave a damn thing out."

His large hand clasps my shoulder. "You make me very proud, Il—Indy. I would be honored. But you will not beat me. Where do you think your skills come from so naturally?"

*S*ix hands in, I'm playing smart and analyzing every man at the table, including my father. Two of them are amateurs with more money than sense, one is a player I decimated in Prague, and the last is Ahmed Al Jabal, the sheikh from the game I played against Forge at La Reina.

Playing in the legendary Casino de Monte Carlo is something I've dreamed about for most of my adult life, but in those dreams, I never once thought I'd play here against my *father*.

But here I am, and here he is.

It takes me four more hands to spot his tell. He's damn good, but his cigar is his downfall. As he bluffs, he rolls it back and forth between his fingers—but only twice.

I push in two stacks of chips. "Call."

Federov's blue eyes cut to mine, and I have to give him credit, there's not a hint or flicker of doubt.

Am I wrong about his tell? No. I don't think so.

We turn over our cards and he grins, even though it's the opposite of the expression he should have. *Because I beat him.*

"Well played," he says as his barrel-shaped chest bounces with silent laughter. "But the night is still young."

Eventually, the tourists drop out of the game, and it's down to me, the sheikh, and my father. The sheikh is holding his own, but he only wins the odd hand. Sooner or later, he will fold and bow out like he did before. That's when things will get serious.

After my father rakes in a pot and a server refreshes our drinks, the dealer stands to be replaced by a new one.

"Perhaps my luck will improve with a new set of hands on the cards," the sheikh says, but then he glances from me to my father, who sits across the table. "Then again, maybe not. I feel like I'm missing something here. Ms. Baptiste, you are playing fiercely tonight."

I've got a lot on the line.

"No more than normal." The lie slips easily off my tongue.

"You've played my daughter before, Ahmed?"

The fact that my father knows the oil billionaire by name should not surprise me, and yet it does. And my father's casual dropping of the bomb regarding our familial relationship to Al Jabal does the same to him.

"Your daughter?" Al Jabal's dark brown eyes dart from my face to my father's. "I had no idea."

It's on the tip of my tongue to say, *I didn't either,* but I keep quiet. My father opened that subject, and therefore he can deal with the fallout.

"Yes, indeed. So please remember that when you're *appreciating her charms.*"

I haven't even noticed the man looking at me. Probably because . . . *I'm blind to other men because of Jericho Forge.* The reminder shifts my determination into overdrive.

All the more reason to win. I miss him, dammit.

With that thought, I lift my club soda and gesture to the sheikh. "Do you want to continue the game, sir? My father and I have a side bet, and I need to warn you, it's going to get ugly."

I throw out the challenge, and my father's grin widens.

With another look between us, Al Jabal pushes back from the table. "I do not like playing games where I am not aware of all the stakes. I shall leave you to your cards. Good luck, Ms. Baptiste. Mr. Federov."

He rises, and when his security rushes forward to collect his remaining chips, it reminds me of Prague when Bates collected mine and then I rushed toward

Jericho, ready for him to pick me up and swing me in the air.

Killing it, Ace. The sound of his voice curls around me, like he's standing right here.

I whip my head around and search the faces in the crowd, but his isn't one of them.

I still have a fighting chance to get him back. There's no way my father will beat me.

It takes another few hands for my father to pick up his cigar from the edge of the table, and as he rolls it between his fingers, he bets big. Goading me. Taunting me. Challenging me.

"Raise," I say, pushing another stack into the center of the green baize that will require him to throw in every single chip he's got on the table.

"You are a ruthless player, Indy," my father says as he calls.

Am I wrong? Did I misjudge? Does he think I'm bluffing?

We flip over our cards, and he throws his head back with a cackling laugh.

I beat him. Soundly.

Slapping his hand on the edge of the table, he shakes his head. "If I had to lose to anyone, daughter, I would prefer it be you."

Triumph dumps into my bloodstream as onlookers applaud, but it's not as sweet as the victories in Prague, because Jericho's not waiting for me with open arms.

But he will be soon, if I have anything to say about it. It's time to get the information I came for.

I toss a high-value chip to the dealer as a tip, rise, and hold my hand out to my father. "Thank you for the game, sir."

He clasps my hand between his two large ones. "It was my pleasure."

"Let's find somewhere to talk. You've got a lot to tell me."

I follow my father to a wood-and-glass-walled smoking room where the only ambient noise is the whir of the ventilation system. Superman and Spiderman wait outside as Federov and I settle into cherry-colored leather chairs.

"How did you know I was bluffing?" he asks as he trims and lights his cigar.

I point at the Cohiba in his hand. "You roll your cigar between your fingers when you're bluffing."

Booming laughter bounces off the walls, and he slaps a hand on his knee. "I should've known better than to give in to my vices. Nothing good ever comes from it for long."

Condensation from my club soda rolls down the sides of the glass as I set it on the table between the arms of our chairs. "Tell me what you said to Forge," I say without preamble.

Federov leans back in his seat and crosses an ankle over one knee. "You are not a patient woman."

"I have a feeling it's an inherited trait."

"You would be right." He lights a match and puffs on the cigar to light it. When an ember burns at the end, he blows out the match and tosses it into an ashtray. "But why do you want to know so badly what was said? Forge gave you up. Why would you want to chase after him?"

Forge gave you up. The wording he uses doesn't sound the same as *kicked you to the curb*, but it still hurts.

"I won, and we had a deal. You don't need to understand any more than that."

He exhales a cloud of smoke, and the air purifiers suck it up toward the ceiling instead of it billowing around my face.

"Do you love him?"

The question hits me hard. Probably harder than it should because this man is a stranger, but he shouldn't be. I share half my DNA with him. Even so, I'm not sure I'm ready to bare my soul to him.

"Does it matter?"

He taps the edge of the cigar on a crystal ashtray before meeting my gaze. "Yes. I think it does."

"Did you love my mother?" I fire back, not wanting to be the only one off-balance here.

"Absolutely."

"Then why did you have a mistress?" The question has been driving me crazy since I learned Nina kidnapped me as a child for revenge.

My father's chin dips, and he focuses on the Aubusson rug on the floor. "To my everlasting regret, I am not a man without faults. It was expected. Encouraged. Almost like a status symbol."

My lips curl in disgust. "Save me from cultures where cheating is fashionable."

"It is hard to explain, Illyana—Indy."

At the sound of my birth name, another question pops into my head. "Did you know she had another daughter? Your mistress?"

"No. When we found her, she gave nothing for information. Just said you were dead. Over and over."

The fact that Nina wouldn't admit I was alive doesn't make sense.

"Why would she lie if she could've saved her life by telling the truth? If you knew her, you'd know that she'd sell out anyone to save her own ass." Bitterness colors my tone, and my father's expression hardens as though he's reliving a memory I don't want to see.

"Nina knew she would die either way. What she did was unforgivable. She held on to her story until the end because she wanted to spite me, even in death."

"You have terrible taste in mistresses, just FYI." I believe his explanation. I've never known a person more selfish than the woman I thought was my mother. It's almost a relief to find out she's not. Still, I have to find a way to tell Summer. She's going to be devastated.

"Was she . . . unkind to you? Did she . . . hurt you?" he asks, and his hesitant tone tells me that he really cares about the answer and is praying that it's not a bad one.

"Nina was indifferent. She didn't beat me or slap me around. She just . . . forced me to grow up really quick. If I wanted to eat, I had to earn it. And then when Summer came along, I had a purpose in life—protect Summer at all costs. There's nothing I wouldn't have done for my sister."

Federov's blue gaze searches my face, and I can only imagine the regret he feels. I don't want to have regrets like that. I don't know how he's survived without them eating away at him every moment of the day. Then again, maybe they have.

"You are a strong woman. I can see why Forge could not resist falling in love with you."

He's the second man to tell me Forge was in love with me, and it packs even more punch this time. I desperately want it to be the truth.

"How . . ." My voice shakes as I try to speak, and I clear my throat to steady it. "How do you know he was falling in love with me?"

My father's hand scoops up his vodka. "Forge did not deny it. And then he let you go."

"But *why*? Why would he let me go? It doesn't make sense. We were fine when we returned to Spain, and then . . . the next day, it was like speaking to a different man. Forge, not Jericho."

My father's jaw shifts at the ragged edge of my tone. "Forge was not a good man, India. He married you because of me. Simply to gain leverage over our deal. Then he put you in more danger because of his feud with de Vere. He left you vulnerable when that danger came to him. The morning after you left Prague, I told him if he had any honor, he would let you go."

Honor? Jericho shattered my heart because of *honor*? The timing of the conversation fits. Everything was great . . . *until my father interfered.* My pulse thrums in my throat. I will never understand men. *Ever.*

"You think he showed honor by letting me go—by doing the right thing. And that makes you believe he loved me?"

My father exhales a cloud of smoke over his right shoulder. "Does it matter? What's done is done."

My fingers sink into the leather arms of my club chair. "It matters because I didn't get a goddamned say. Did you ever stop to think that I might want him, whether you thought he had honor or not? Did it ever occur to you that I might be in love with him?"

A shadow passes over my father's face. "I do not

want to see you upset. That was not my goal. But . . . there are things you still don't understand."

"What?"

He puffs on the cigar before he speaks. "I told Forge that giving you up forever was the only way I would agree to sign his deal with Karas and Riscoff."

My entire body tenses. "When? What did he say?"

"I cannot tell you. I swore to him I would not."

*T*he report comes in, and I grin for the first time in weeks.

SMITH: *Indy beat her father at poker in Monte Carlo.*

OF COURSE SHE DID. Because that's my girl. My smile dies as quickly as it came. *Except she's not. Not anymore.*

I walk away from the bridge and outside into the wind whipping the Atlantic into six-to-eight-foot swells. I text back.

. . .

FORGE: Keep her safe. If anything happens to her, it's your head on the chopping block.

SMITH: Yes, sir. Understood. She's more cooperative now than she was. We'll stay close.

FORGE: You better. Where is she now?

SMITH: Leaving her father. We're on it.

I STARE at the screen of my phone, wishing that I were the one standing there, watching her. Close to her.

Fuck. I'm a pathetic piece of shit. I gave her up. Ran her out. Fucking broke her goddamned heart. I don't deserve another glimpse at paradise.

I jam the phone in my pocket and trudge back down to the engine room to take over for whoever is cleaning the bilge.

My penance. But it'll never be enough.

INDIA

*a*s I walked away from my father in Monte Carlo, he tried to talk me into returning to Russia with him and forgetting Forge. I refused.

I still remember his stubborn expression as he said, *"You will come. You must learn things . . . before it is too late."*

He wouldn't tell me why it would be too late, so I left him with a promise that I would think about it.

He didn't like that at all.

I departed Monte Carlo the next morning, eager to get home, because there was nothing else to learn in Monaco. A few hours after touching down, I'm already forming phase two of my plan. A knock comes on my door, and I freeze.

"Ms. Baptiste, your sister would like to see you,"

Superman says through the door, where he is determined to stand all day.

After placing my espresso on the counter, I cross the room to unbolt my locks.

To distract myself from thoughts of Jericho during my sleepless night in Monte Carlo, I went through option after option for telling Summer about her mother and my father. I can't keep it from her much longer, but I still don't know how to tell her without breaking her heart.

As soon as I open the door, her red-rimmed eyes track over my face. I glance at Superman, but he shrugs as if to say, *I have no idea what's wrong with her.*

"What did you say to her, Indy? Seriously? Could you not just let me have this one thing?" Summer swipes at a tear that falls, smearing her mascara across her cheek.

"What are you talking about? Are you okay? What happened?"

My protective instincts rage to the forefront as I pull her inside, but Summer snatches her arm from my grip with an accusing stare.

"Don't act like you don't know."

"Know what? Tell me. Please." Concern edges my tone, and I hate that I can't reach out to her and fix whatever's wrong. I close the door behind her as she marches into the living room.

"I got thrown out on my ass this morning when I

showed up for work. Juliette was out of town yesterday, but she came in this morning and fired me and made this awful scene. She called me a whore like my sister."

Oh, that bitch.

A cold calmness settles over me. "I am so sorry, Summer."

"You should be! Now I'm never going to have a career in the fashion industry because she said she's going to blackball me with every label on the planet." Summer bursts into full-blown sobs.

I rush toward her and wrap my arms around her shaking shoulders, not caring if she wants my comfort or not. "I'm so sorry. I saw her in Monte Carlo. We had words. I didn't even think—"

"About me?" She jerks away from me. "Of course you didn't. Because what do I matter?"

My sister's despair kills me. "I'm so sorry. You always matter. You know that. If you didn't, I wouldn't have married a stranger to save your life."

"Don't pretend that was for me! You wanted him anyway!"

Her anger hits me even harder, but it forces me to ask myself the question. *Had I wanted him no matter what, then?*

I was slightly terrified, yet intrigued, by Forge when he threw down his proposal in the form of a no-questions-asked favor. Under any other circumstances, I would have told him to shove the proposal up his ass. I did marry him for Summer, but that's not why I wanted to *stay married to him.*

But he let me go . . . to be honorable. Because he didn't let me choose. He forced my hand. And then he let me go, even though . . . he might have been falling in love with me.

Maybe we didn't start out the right way, but that doesn't matter to me anymore. All that matters is what happens *now.*

"See, I'm right," my sister says when I don't reply. She's completely unaware of the epiphany I'm having.

"I'm sorry, Summer. Truly. Completely. What can I do to fix this for you?"

"You can't." She lifts her chin, her lips wobbling as she holds back a sob. "But Forge could. Juliette would listen to him if he told her not to blackball me."

"If that's what you want, that's what will happen."

Summer's platinum-blond brows wing up. "How? You said he threw you out. It's already *over,* Indy. God, Juliette loved rubbing it in my face."

"It's not over. Not until I say it's over." I straighten my shoulders and shore up my emotions. "I'll marry Jericho again tomorrow if I have to. But first, I have to find him and explain to him exactly why he doesn't get to make decisions about our future without involving me."

Summer steps back on a wobbling heel. "Whoa. Really?"

"Yes. Really. And so what if you got fired? Start your own damn fashion label. Make what you want. Fuck everyone else. That's how we work in this family, Summer."

My sister's anger drains away to be replaced by an expression of open-mouthed wonderment. "Really?"

"If that's what you want. I'll be your investor. But you have to promise me you'll take it seriously."

Summer's big blue eyes shine with glee instead of tears. "I will. I swear. I really will. Juliette doesn't know it, but I studied everything she did—and I can do it better. I just need a splashy way to enter the market. Something daring and incredible."

"We'll come up with something," I tell her. "Start working on your business plan. I have calls to make."

Leaving my sister inside with a bracing cup of tea, I step out onto the balcony with my phone and make a call to one person who might actually be able to help me.

"Indy? Is that you?" Holly answers the phone on the second ring.

"Thank you so much for taking my call. I know you're busy." I stare out at the birds swooping across the blue sky and sit on a cushioned chaise.

"Anytime. I told you, we're friends. What can I do for you?" The background noise, people yelling and instruments playing, fades away.

"I didn't have Creighton's number, but I need some information, and I was hoping you could help me."

"He's backstage with me, actually. What do you need to know?"

"That deal with my father. Did it go through?"

"You're going to want to talk to him. Hold on a sec."

Her voice grows faint as she explains who is on the phone before she hands off the call.

"India, it's Creighton Karas."

"I need some information. Really, I just need to know about the deal with my father and what's happening."

There's a silence on the line before he answers. "The deal is off."

His clipped tone tells me there's a hell of a lot more to it, but a tendril of hope rises up from the cracks in my soul.

"Really? Why? What happened?" I ask as I rise from the chaise to pace my small balcony.

"I'm not at liberty to say."

"Creighton. Please. I saw my father in Monte Carlo. He said he made the ultimatum that he would only close the deal if Forge agreed to give me up forever."

"Goddamned Russian. I knew there was something going on that didn't make sense. Forge wouldn't sign off, even when your father agreed to revert to the original agreement and drop the clause about giving him—and eventually you—a share in the new company."

He wouldn't agree to give me up. That tendril of hope blooms inside me like a field of sunflowers reaching for the sky. *He does care. There's hope still.*

"I'm sorry, Creighton. I really am. Kind of. I need to find my husband." I squeeze one hand into a fist as I wait for him to give me the information I need.

"Indy . . . I hate to tell you this, but I'm pretty sure you're not married anymore."

"I've heard," I tell him as the sun warms my face. I'm not even upset about being divorced now. *Not when Jericho refused to say he'd give me up forever.* "Which is why I need to find him."

Creighton is quiet for a few moments, and when he speaks, his tone is contemplative. "I wish he would've told me what was going on. We could've found a way to make this work. Riscoff might never speak to Forge again after this stunt, and our friendship took a huge hit."

"I think I might be able to fix things."

"What can I do to help?" Creighton asks, and I want to hug him.

"Do you know where Jericho is?"

"No idea. The last time I talked to him, the connection was shit and he was calling from a sat phone, so I'm assuming out to sea on one of his cargo ships. If I were you, I'd ask his employees. They're going to have a better idea."

"Okay. I can work with that. I'll be in touch. Thanks, Creighton."

"Good luck, Indy. And for what it's worth, I'm glad you're fighting for him. I don't think anyone ever has."

When I end the call, I know exactly what I'm going to do next.

Jericho Forge doesn't have a single clue what it's like to be the center of someone's world. He's about to find out.

But first . . . I have to lure him back to Isla del Cielo.

34

FORGE

"What the fuck do you mean, *she's on the island*?"

"Sir, we didn't know what to do. Smith and Sanderson are here with her. Do you want me to have them remove her?" Dorsey asks.

The one damn time I leave my phone in my cabin, all hell breaks loose, in the form of India showing up on Isla del Cielo, unannounced.

I jam a hand into my hair, shifting my weight to steady myself as the ocean rages around us. The Atlantic's got nothing on the emotions boiling over inside me.

"What is she trying to accomplish with this?" I ask myself the question more than Dorsey.

"She told Smith and Sanderson she wanted to check on Goliath. That's why they agreed to bring her out. But she brought a bag, sir, and she put it in a guest room like she plans on staying here."

Her actions make no sense. *What the hell is going through Indy's mind?*

"Sir?" Dorsey asks. "Do you want me to remove her?"

I think of the deal I killed because I refused to promise Federov I would never go near India again. The ruthless businessman I've always been would have had no problem making that vow because the potential profit should have eclipsed every other consideration.

But for the first time in my life, something was more important than closing a deal. *Someone.* When I pictured living the rest of my life without seeing or touching India Baptiste, it stretched out before me like a wasteland. No meaning. No purpose. Just yawning emptiness.

In my whole life, she's the one thing I want more than the satisfaction of winning.

I told Federov to shove his ultimatum up his ass. I would never agree to his terms, and the deal could go to hell.

It was the right choice. The only choice.

And now Indy's in my home. Making herself at home.

Hope, something I've never let into my life before, weaves its way into my soul. *The same way Indy did.*

"No. Don't make her leave. Watch her, though. Find out what she wants."

"Yes, sir."

"And, Dorsey?"

"Yes?"

"Don't tell her you called me."

"Of course, sir."

As soon as I end the call, I head out to the deck to suck in fresh air and stare up at the sky above me. The salt spray in the air clings to my face as I thank whoever's listening for giving me a second chance.

My next message goes to the helicopter pilot with our current coordinates.

FORGE: Get me off the boat as fast as fucking possible.

THE *FORTUNA*, one of Isaac's first cargo ships, used to be the place I felt most at home. The only place I could find any comfort, because I could feel Isaac's presence here more than anywhere else in the world.

But not anymore. I have a life to get back to . . . and a woman to claim as my own. Come hell or high water, if she'll have me, I'm never giving her up again.

India . . . I hope you're ready, because everything I am, and everything I have, is yours. Including my heart.

*T*he staff gape at me like I've lost my mind, but I feel like I've finally found it. I know what matters, and I know what I truly want. For my entire life, I've been fiercely loyal to my family, or at least the family I knew. Since Isaac's death, Forge hasn't had a single person who wasn't on his payroll to care about him.

Whatever it takes, that ends now.

I'm setting up for a game on the poker table I had delivered from La Reina, a favor I called in from Jean Phillippe. To his credit, he didn't ask many questions.

"Ms. Baptiste . . ." Dorsey has been hovering around me like she's afraid I'm on the scary end of a mental break and is waiting for me to snap at any moment.

Her concern is misplaced. I'm not losing my mind . . . I've finally found it.

"Indy. I told you to call me Indy."

She clears her throat. "Okay. Indy, do you really think this is a good idea?"

I straighten the final stack of chips and stand back to inspect my handiwork before I turn to answer her. She's dressed in the same uniform of white slacks and navy polo with the stylized *F* on the breast as she usually wears.

"What's your first name, Dorsey?"

The woman blinks, looking shocked that I would ask such a question. "Darcy."

"Darcy Dorsey? Really?"

Her teeth scrape over her bottom lip before she answers. "I wasn't always a Dorsey. It was my stepfather's name. I took it when he adopted me in hopes that he wouldn't knock me around as much if he thought of me as his kid."

"I'm so sorry," I whisper, wishing I hadn't brought up the subject.

"It's over and done with. Not important anymore." But her tone says that's not true.

"It is important. Old hurts . . . they stick with us. I'm going to get real for a second with you. I make a lot of mistakes. I'm rash. Impulsive. Overconfident one minute and terrified the next. I learned to survive because I had to. I fuck things up as often as I get them right. But I know when to admit I'm wrong, and I should never have signed those divorce papers. I love Jericho Forge, and I'm not giving up on him."

Her lips, devoid of any gloss or color, press together. "I understand what you're saying, but Jericho Forge isn't a man who can be swayed to do something he doesn't want to do. I like you, Indy. But I don't want you to get your hopes up that this is going to work out. Once he's made up his mind, he doesn't change it."

Hearing something so grave from his employee's lips doesn't help my confidence, but it doesn't lessen my resolve either. I knew the odds would be stacked against me, and I can handle it. Nothing worth having ever comes easily.

"I'm willing to take my chances. Will you help me?"

Dorsey peers off into the distance as she considers my request. Then her gaze swings back to me. "What do you need me to do?"

FORGE

When I climb the steps of the cliff face, the sky is dark from the raging storm. The ride in on the chopper was rough, and we were forced to land at the airport rather than on Isla del Cielo. The rain beat down on me the entire boat ride out here, but nothing short of the apocalypse could keep me away.

Dorsey called to warn me that Indy planned a massive poker game to take place *on my island*. I don't know what the hell she's thinking, but it's not happening without me.

When I tied up the tender at the dock, it was empty but for the other runabout we use for errands. If there's supposed to be a giant game, where the fuck is everyone?

Did they all get ferried out and dropped off? Or did the weather keep them away?

I hurry up the stairs, and when I reach the top of the cliff, the house is lit up like it's welcoming me home. *And it was home, until I threw Indy out.*

What is going through that brilliant mind of hers?

I slip inside quietly, my hair hanging wet against my face from charging the boat through the rising waves. Instead of hearing laughter and the chatter of guests in my house, I find it completely silent.

Did Dorsey lie to me? What the hell is going on?

I stride into the living room, and there's a poker table set up where a table with a bronze Henry Moore sculpture used to sit. Two chairs sit on either side of it, and they're both empty.

What the fuck?

Is this an intimate game for two? Who the hell is she playing? Jealousy crashes through me like a tsunami. *I have no right to be jealous. I gave her up. I tore us apart.*

But she came to *me. To my house.* That has to mean something.

"I wondered how long you'd keep me waiting, Jericho."

My head swivels toward Indy's voice. She leans a shoulder against the archway to the kitchen. She stands casually, like she's not every man's fantasy come to life in that gold dress she tossed in my face that first night at La Reina.

Goddammit. She looks fucking beautiful. Her cheekbones are sharper than they were before, and her curves aren't as voluptuous.

Was she not eating? Why didn't they tell me? Why didn't her mom and sister make sure she was taking care of herself?

"Nothing to say?"

I tear my gaze off the details I'm memorizing. *Why the fuck did I listen to her father? Why did I give a shit about honor?*

My hands flex, needing to touch her. Being so close to her and not being able to pull her against me is fucking torture.

"What are you doing here?" My voice comes out low and harsh. I sound like a man dying for his last glimpse at the woman he could have had but gave up . . . in an attempt to be noble.

"I liked your island. It felt like home. At least, it did until I came back and you weren't here."

The knot in my chest that's been strangling me for weeks loosens a fraction. *Why is she here? What is her plan?* I glance at the poker table, with cards in the center and chips stacked in front of both chairs.

"So you came back and decided to redecorate?" My question is cautious, because I'm not sure how this is going to go down.

A secretive smile stretches over her ruby-slicked lips. Lips I'd cut off my right fucking arm to be able to kiss again.

She pushes off the archway and strides toward the table, and my nails dig into my palms when I get a good, long look at her legs. *Fuck, but I missed those legs.*

Who am I kidding? There's not a single fucking piece of her mind, body, or soul I haven't missed.

"I don't know if you've heard, but they're calling me the best poker player in Europe . . . but I don't feel like I truly claim the title yet."

"What do you mean?"

Indy stops on the other side of the table, behind the chair. "Because you beat me, and I want a rematch. That's the only way I'll know I'm the best."

The hope growing inside me disappears like a ship in the fog. "That's what this is about? You went through all this trouble . . . to *prove you're the best*?"

Her smile turns predatory as she grips the wooden back of the chair. "Also because it'll be financially *beneficial* to me."

Indy throws my own words at me, and I stare at her as my brain races. *This isn't about a poker game. This is about us.*

"Financially beneficial. Sounds familiar."

"So, what do you say? Will you play me?" The question carries a wealth of challenge.

I walk around the table, past the seat I assume is mine, and she releases her grip on hers as I close the distance between us. I grasp the back of her chair and pull it out, leaning forward to inhale her scent. *Citrus and sun and sea.* It makes me go hard as a rock as I meet her gaze.

"I'll accept any challenge you throw at me, India. If you want to play, we play."

*W*hen he stops beside me, I almost lose my composure.

There's nothing I want to do more than throw myself at him and tell him I don't give a fuck about titles or games or anything but him, but I can't. I have a plan, and I'm going to follow it.

Coyly, I look up at Jericho, my ex-husband, from under my lashes. "Thank you. You're the gentleman tonight."

He breathes in deeply, like a predator would scent its prey, as I lower myself into my seat and he pushes it in.

"I guess we'll see if you're right or wrong about that," Jericho says as he backs away. "I'm definitely underdressed for this game." He motions to his work pants, boots, and rain jacket, and then to my dress.

"I don't mind, if you don't."

For the first time, I'm seeing the man beneath all the expensive clothes and veneer of sophistication. Jericho Forge ruthlessly carved out a place for himself in the world, and he didn't do it wearing custom-made suits and expensive watches. However, he never showed that side to me, and I love seeing it.

"Fair enough." He pulls out his own chair and sits down, glancing at the chips in front of him.

"I haven't bought in yet."

"Don't worry, I fronted you the stake." I smile, because the tables are once again turning, and if everything goes according to plan, I will win *him* tonight.

*S*he's a siren, and I'm the sailor she's trying to lure in. I've never wrecked a ship, but she could tempt me to do anything.

I may not be good enough for her or deserve her, but I will spend a lifetime learning to be the man she needs me to be.

"It seems we're short a dealer," I say, pointing to the deck of cards in the middle of the table.

"I thought we'd take turns. That is . . . if you trust me."

Just like earlier, every word that comes out of her mouth carries a double meaning.

"That depends. Do you trust me?" I ask.

"With my life."

Indy's declaration hits me hard, and the knot in my chest loosens another degree, allowing hope to rekindle.

"You're not worried I'll deal from the bottom? Cheat to win?" I can't stop myself from asking the question, because we both know I technically cheated to win her before.

Indy smiles, and it's like watching the sunrise after a year of darkness. "You want to play dirty? Bring it on. I'm not scared of you, Forge."

She's my equal in every way. More than I ever thought I could have. If this is my only chance at happiness, I won't waste it.

A wolfish grin tugs at my lips. "Get ready, Ace. I'm playing for keeps."

"*O*h, we're playing for keeps, all right. I'm going to own *you* when we're done." My cocky attitude barely covers the hammering of my heart.

I'm trying not to read into everything he says, but I can't help it. My pulse is racing and my palms are sweaty. I can't lose my composure before we even start.

I take a deep breath and reach across the table for the cards, careful to allow him a long look down the neckline of my dress. I'm brazen enough to even hope I flash a little nipple. *I'm not above playing dirty either.*

In my head, I've worked out exactly how I want tonight to end. With us, naked on the table, Jericho buried inside me where he belongs—until he finally admits that he loves me and can't live without me.

When I told him that I thought this island felt like home, I meant it—as long as he's here. Without him, it's just another place filled with memories that aren't enough to satisfy me. I'm greedy, and I make no apologies for it. I want him, and I want him *forever*.

"You seem to have forgotten some lingerie, India."

I wink as I lower back into my seat, not caring that my dress is riding up. "Indy. My friends call me *Indy*."

Jericho's dark brows rise toward his wet hair. "Are we friends?"

"I think we will be by the end of the night." I tap the tip of my tongue to the back of my front teeth, and Jericho shifts in his seat. *Please, God, let him be as desperate for me as I am for him.*

"Are you trying to distract me, *Indy*?" He leans back in his chair, unzipping his rain jacket.

"I don't have to try, *Jericho*. I succeed." My confidence is growing by leaps and bounds, because he's giving me every reason to hope that everything I want is everything *he wants*.

He shrugs out of the jacket and hangs it on the chair behind him. Beneath it, a damp white T-shirt sticks to his skin.

"How are you wet *under* your rain jacket?"

"I got caught in the rain getting out of the chopper. Wasn't prepared until I got to the boat."

I swallow a lump in my throat as I stare at the outline of his shoulders, pecs, and abs. He's the most beautiful man I've ever seen.

"Do you want to change into a dry shirt?" I say, sounding like a frog took up residence in my throat.

"Not unless you've changed your mind about being okay with taking me as I am."

I press my lips together, hauling back the urge to vault over the table, climb onto his lap and tell him I will take him any way I can get him, and forget this entire freaking game. *But I have willpower,* I remind myself. *And a point to prove and a promise to extract.*

"You don't have to change a single thing for me. I just don't want you to be uncomfortable."

His gaze drops to his lap. "I'm uncomfortable, all right, but it's not because of my wet shirt."

This motherfucker. God, he's sexy.

Never before has the prelude to a poker game been the best foreplay of my entire life. My thighs press together, but my lack of panties means that my skin is slick with my own arousal.

I'm going to ride him all night long—after I win.

"Then by all means, get comfortable."

His stormy gaze bores into me. "Oh, I plan to. Deal the cards, Indy. I'm ready to play."

*H*ow could I have ever walked away from this woman? *Temporary insanity.*

If being honorable means living without her, honor can go to hell. I can't walk away from her again. I'll take whatever she's prepared to offer me tonight and never let go.

"Blinds," Indy says as she pushes in a stack of $100,000 chips.

"Playing deep tonight."

Her blue eyes spark with challenge. "That's the only way I like it."

Fucking siren. Lure me in. I push double the amount of chips in for the big blind.

Her delicate hands deftly shuffle the cards, and she deals the hole cards from the top, at least as far as I can tell because she's quick as fuck.

I didn't check the decks for markings, because if she wants to cheat to win, I'm not going to complain. She's here to make some kind of point, hopefully to save what I fucked up so badly.

Eagerly, I reach for the two cards in front of me and slide them toward me facedown. My brain is running a thousand miles an hour, and I barely remember how to play poker at this point.

I'm tempted to throw the game, but I suspect that's not what she wants. We'll go head-to-head, toe-to-toe, and then I'm going to beg for forgiveness and promise her a future that's beyond anything she can imagine.

For weeks, I've been drifting without purpose, and nothing could hold my attention. I didn't give a fuck about work, about life, about anything. Because without her . . . I'm a shell of a man. But in her presence, I can slay dragons.

Indy lifts the edges of the two cards in front of her enough to see what they are, and I do the same. *Nine of hearts and eight of hearts.*

With a glance across the table at her, I can't help but wonder what she's holding. Although that thought is a far distant second to all of the things I want to do to her right now. Peel that dress from her body, find out what she's wearing beneath it, if anything.

The thought sends the remaining blood in my body to my dick. I can't concentrate, and it's even worse when she smiles at me from across the table.

Whatever she's holding is good.

Or she's got me so mixed up, I don't know how to do anything but stare at her.

Indy pushes chips into the center of the table, and without a second thought, I shove two stacks forward. I don't count or care. One hand. That's all this game is going to last, because everything I need is sitting on the other side of the green baize. She's the one thing money can't buy, and she's my fucking world.

Indy looks up at me, and I hope like hell we're on the same wavelength here.

"Bold," she murmurs, rolling a chip across her knuckles. She burns the top card before dealing the flop.

Jack of hearts. Ace of diamonds. Nine of spades.

Indy bets first, and I watch for her tell, but I spot nothing. I call, barely paying attention as she tosses another card aside.

The turn comes next. *Queen of hearts.* We both check.

Last burned card.

Finally, she lays the river on the table between us. *Ten of hearts.*

I have a straight flush.

Indy watches while I lay my hands on the rest of my chips and shove them toward the center.

"I'm all in, Ace."

She looks up at me, her indigo gaze searching my face. For what, though, I'm not sure.

"But are you really?"

I stare at the woman across from me, the only woman I've loved enough to try to be a better man. Whatever she wants from me, she'll get.

"What do you mean?" I ask, because I need to make sure I understand her question.

"You held back before, and then you wrecked me, Jericho. I've never felt loss like I did when you threw me out of your life as if I meant nothing to you." All playfulness is gone, and her eyes shimmer with tears. "You decided my future without even asking what *I* wanted or how I felt."

My head dips under the weight of my shame.

"You pushed me away. Made me think I was nothing to you."

My hands clench into fists, and my own vision blurs with unshed tears. "I don't deserve you, India. I've never deserved you. I *will never* deserve you. Even when I tried to do the right thing . . . all I did was hurt you."

I look up at her as she drops the chip.

"But I will never let you go again, as long as there's breath in my body. Honor can go to hell. All I want out of this life is *you*. I love you, India, and if I could, I'd rip my heart from my chest and put it on this table, because it's yours. But all I have is this."

I fish her diamond ring out of my pocket, where I've kept it for weeks after she threw it at me in my study the day I told her to go. My heart in my throat, I lay the ring on the table between us.

Indy's lips press together, and a single tear spills over her lashes.

"Then it's a really good fucking thing that I'm winning this game." She flips her cards over to reveal the ace and king of hearts before snatching the ring off the green baize. "Because I'm never taking it off again."

INDIA

As soon as the ring is on my finger, Jericho surges from his chair and charges around the table to lift me out of mine. Our lips meet in a chaotically beautiful collision. His hands roam over my arms, around my back, under my ass, like he can't stop touching me. Can't believe I'm real and here.

I tear my lips away from his for a second to tell him something I've never said to a man. "I love you, Jericho. So damn much. Don't you ever try to push me away again."

"Never again. I swear it. I love you, Indy."

He lays me out on the table and pulls the straps of the gold dress down my shoulders. My breasts spill free and his mouth skims along their curves, raising chill bumps in its wake. "I need you. All of you."

"That's what you get. Every heartbeat. Every

fucking breath. Everything I am and everything I have is yours."

One hand slides beneath my dress and finds the slickness coating my thighs. Jericho groans against my mouth before he pauses.

"I'll buy you a new dress."

"What—"

Before I can get the question out, he tears the fabric down the center, baring me completely. The dress I once considered unlucky has turned into the luckiest of my life. But I don't need luck now, because I've got everything I could ever want.

My greedy fingers snatch at the buttons of his pants, and I wrench them open. As soon as he's free, he pushes between my thighs, and the head of his cock nudges against my entrance.

Jericho pauses before he presses inside. "I want a family. At least two kids. More, if you want." His voice is rough and ragged with emotion.

A family.

"Yes," I whisper. "I want that too."

With a buck of his hips, Jericho powers inside me, and my muscles tense as he stretches me wide. He owns me. My body. My heart. My soul.

Thrust after thrust, I cling to him as he takes me higher and closer to the edge. My nails dig into his shoulders as I lift my hips to meet every stroke.

It wasn't the island that was home. It's the man.

"I love you," I scream as my control snaps and my orgasm sweeps me away. Jericho wraps his arms around me and holds me close as his body pulses his climax.

"I love you, India. So fucking much."

*W*hen I wake up, I'm scared I'll find an empty bed, and last night will be nothing but a dream. But the twinges of my body and the massive source of heat pressed beside me tell me that I'm wrong on both counts. *Thankfully.*

I roll over to see dark hair spread across the pillow and his tanned hand only inches from my face.

I never gave him a ring. This time, that's going to change.

In the rush of last night, I never actually asked if the divorce proceedings were final. But if there's one thing I've learned in the last month, a piece of paper doesn't mean jack shit when it comes to love. You're either all in or you're not, and even if we're not married anymore, it changes nothing about how I feel and the direction of our future.

When Jericho's lids pop open, his gray eyes are less stormy this morning. Now they're more the dark silver of a clouded moon reflecting off the ocean, and they're absolutely beautiful.

"You're here." His voice comes out sleep-roughened.

"Did you think I wouldn't be?" I ask, sliding my fingers down his heavily muscled arm.

The hand nearest my face rises, and he trails two fingers across my cheek. "I thought I'd wake up and this would all be a dream."

A smile tugs at my lips. "I thought the same thing."

"Best damn dream of my life, though. I never want to wake up from this, Indy." His palm curls around my cheek and his fingers tuck into my hair. "Kiss me so I know you're real."

"Morning breath—"

"Don't fucking care."

Jericho's lips sweep over mine, and his tongue slides inside. He wraps his arm around me and pulls me closer to his chest. Skin against skin, he kisses me like I'm the most essential thing in the world. More important than time or money or goddamned oxygen.

When he finally pulls back, those gray eyes turn solemn. "No more games. No more deals. We're going to talk. Communicate. When things go wrong or something's bothering you, you tell me. I tell you. No more surprises. We're still going to fight, because we're both hardheaded as hell, but then we're going to make up, and it's going to be fucking worth it."

"I like the sound of that."

"Good, because I'm not here to tell you how to live your life. I just want to be the lucky son of a bitch who gets to be part of it every day."

A burst of warmth gusts through me and I squeeze him tighter. "I love you."

"Good, because you're stuck with me."

I lift up to meet his gaze. "You're supposed to say you love me too."

"I love you more than life itself. If you needed an arm, I'd offer mine up, no matter how strange it would look attached to your body. You're it for me, Indy."

His starkly handsome face, with his dark five o'clock shadow, is completely serious, and my heart feels like it might burst open from joy.

"I love you," I whisper again, this time with tears leaking from the corners of my eyes.

"Ace, you can't cry now. It kills me."

"They're happy tears," I say as he carefully wipes them away.

"I should've made a no-crying rule when I had the chance," he says in a grumble, but it's halfhearted at best. "Come on. I'm going to make you breakfast."

I roll over onto my back and stare up at the ceiling. "And he cooks," I whisper. "Luckiest. Woman. Ever."

Jericho's laugh echoes through the bedroom as he reaches for my hand to pull me out of bed.

*I*f losing Isaac taught me anything, it was that life is short. Tomorrow isn't a guarantee. Somehow, in the midst of all of this, I forgot how important it is not to waste a single day, because you don't know when your number will be up.

As Indy and I dress and walk out into the kitchen hand in hand, I make a promise to myself. *Treat her like I'm going to lose her tomorrow.* There's nothing like the imminent possibility of losing the person you love most to make you appreciate her even more.

I have more money than I could spend in three lifetimes, and revenge . . . well, I already learned that isn't satisfying when it costs you everything that matters.

The kitchen is empty when we arrive, and I silently thank Dorsey for giving us space. She and the others are hopefully holed up on the back side of the island in the staff houses.

"You, stool." I point Indy to the bar on the opposite side of the massive granite-topped island in the kitchen that houses the stove top and a sink.

"You don't have to tell me twice. Everything tastes doubly good when I don't have to cook it for myself. Or burn it for myself . . . as the case may be."

She twists her messy hair up into a knot on her head, and the memory of her telling me she was high maintenance and didn't wake up looking gorgeous comes back. *She lied.* She looks even more beautiful this morning than she did last night.

I reach into the fridge for the ingredients to make scrambled eggs and pancakes from scratch. The chef on board the *Fortuna* didn't mind me hanging out in the kitchen as a kid, especially since my ribs practically poked through my skin during those early weeks after I stowed away.

"I'll teach you," I tell her.

Indy's grin turns wry. "That may be an impossible task."

"Never. Now, watch and learn."

I open the drawers in the island for the dry goods and measure them in a bowl before mixing them up and adding in all the wet ingredients, including a healthy dash of vanilla. Before I whisk, I grab an orange, wash it, and scrape some zest into the mixture.

"Now I can say I've seen it all. Jericho Forge knows how to use kitchen utensils I've never seen, but I'm pretty sure you just zested an orange."

"That's the secret ingredient. Now you really can't escape, because I can't take a chance that you'll spill." Even though my words are joking, Indy's smile dies. "What?"

"You know I'd never tell anyone anything you tell me. About you, your business, your life . . ."

My head jerks back at her quiet statement. "You don't need to say that. I trust you, India. With my life."

Her smile comes back. "Then we're even, because my heart's in your hands. Take care of it."

I walk around the counter to pull her into my arms. "You have my solemn vow."

Breakfast has to wait another hour, because I carry her back to the bedroom.

"Sir? I don't want to interrupt, but we have someone requesting permission to land."

"Permission to land?" Indy asks, looking up from her pancakes, which are now brunch.

"Who?" I ask Sanderson, lowering my fork.

"Grigory Federov. They're two minutes out."

Nothing he can say will make me give her up. Not a

fucking thing. It's time to make sure the Russian understands.

"Grant permission."

"I can't believe he's here." Indy sounds just as shocked as she looks. "He was just in Monaco . . . why would he come here? I beat him, you know."

"I heard. I was proud as hell."

"That's when he told me what he said to you. Why you pushed me away."

Regret rolls through me. I hate that I let Federov get in my head and force me to make a decision I didn't want to make. But he was right in some respects. I didn't start things with Indy the right way, and if what we have is going to stand the test of a lifetime, it needs a solid foundation. That foundation has been laid, whether he likes it or not.

"He had his reasons," I tell her. "But it'll never happen again."

"Why didn't you close the deal you were making with him? I know he offered you what you wanted."

From inside the house, the *whap-whap-whap* of the rotors grows louder as the chopper approaches the island.

"Then you also know why I couldn't close it. I couldn't give him the promise he wanted in return."

"To give me up forever." Indy's pained gaze locks onto mine.

"I could never agree to that." I thread my fingers

through hers on the counter. "Not for all the money in the world."

"Even if your partners were pissed the deal fell through?"

"They'll live. Nothing is more important than you."

A hint of mischief winks in her blue eyes as she presses her lips to mine. "I think we can have it all, and that's exactly what I'm going to tell my father."

I've never been a businesswoman. A gambler, yes. But a legitimate businesswoman? Not exactly. I'm still about to facilitate a business deal, though, because it's time.

Federov may never have the daughter he wants at home in Russia, but I'm hoping we can find a way to have a relationship, and for Jericho and his partners to get what they need from him.

Jericho goes outside to meet the chopper, and a few minutes later, he leads my father inside. Kostya waits just beyond the door. The older man's face creases in surprise, his eyebrows going up, when he sees me sitting in the kitchen.

"You . . . you're here. With him. How?"

I walk toward him. "You told me what I needed to know. I made my decision."

My father glances from me to Jericho. There's no mistaking that we're having a cozy meal for two.

"Then my presence is *de trop*, I assume," he says, shoving his hands into his pockets.

"Why are you here?" I ask.

"I wanted to tell Forge that I was wrong to interfere. I shouldn't have said what I said. I was an old man protecting his daughter, and after many years of being denied such a privilege, I may have been overzealous in my approach."

"No," Jericho says, surprising me. "You weren't. Things needed to be said."

"That is good you agree," my father says.

"But if you ever try to meddle again, all bets are off," I tell him.

My father gives me a look of respect. "Point taken."

"One more thing," I say. "You're signing the deal. Original terms. No more bullshit. I won't be used as a pawn in anyone's game ever again."

Jericho turns to stare at me in surprise, but my father just smiles. "Fine. Bring the contract. But I do have one condition." He pulls a pen out of his jacket pocket.

I tilt my head to the left. "And what's that?"

"I do want to be part of your life, Ill—India. For what little time I have left."

I blink. "What . . . what do you mean?"

"I'm ill. The doctors say I do not have many months to live."

"I . . . I didn't know. I'm . . . sorry." My words come out stilted.

He's dying? How is that possible? Why didn't he tell me before? His ruddy face shows signs of hard living, but nothing of the gaunt paleness I would associate with being terminally ill. *I just found out I have a father, and now I'm going to lose him.*

"There is no need to be sorry. I have lived a long life, and my final wish has been granted." He walks toward me and takes my hand. "All I wanted was to tell you that you have always been loved, whether you were with me or not."

I squeeze his much larger hand with both of mine. "Thank you."

"No, thank you. I am very proud of the woman you have become, even if I did not have a hand in it."

I swallow the lump in my throat as he lifts my hand to press a kiss to the back. "Your mother would be proud as well. Now, let us get the contract signed, and we shall toast the beginning of a new venture. One that, hopefully, my grandchildren will oversee someday."

My gaze collides with Jericho's, and he smiles. "I can toast to that."

*R*iscoff and Karas sign off on the agreement as soon as I tell them the deal's back on. Indy, her father, and I sit out near the deck of the pool. As he tells her about his home in Russia, Dorsey refreshes our coffee.

"I would like you to see it someday. After all, it will all be yours," Federov says. When I shoot him a sharp look, not wanting him to pressure her, he adds, "But it will be managed easily until you decide it is time. I have a board of directors who have the power to oversee everything, and all profits flow into a trust for you if they are not reinvested in the company."

Indy looks a little overwhelmed, but she's rolling with it. "I don't know anything about steel, or . . . what else do you do?"

The older man laughs, and it's still hard to believe

he's dying. He looks healthier than most men his age. Before I can think further on that, a boat catches my attention as it roars toward the dock.

A red boat. Bastien's boat.

I jolt out of my seat as the boat closes in on the island.

"What's wrong?" Indy pops out of her chair, her blond hair swirling around her face.

"We have an unwelcome visitor. Stay here." I pull out my phone, but Sanderson is already jogging toward the edge of the cliff.

"I'll handle it, sir."

"I'm coming with you," I tell him.

"Jericho? What's going on?" Indy's knuckles are white where she grips the back of her chair.

"I think Bastien de Vere has finally lost his fucking mind," I tell her before I run toward Sanderson as he disappears down the stairs.

"Let me—"

I turn around to see Indy following me. "Stay here."

I know she wants to argue, but all she says is, "Promise me you'll be careful."

"I swear. Wait with your dad. I'll be back."

By the time I make it to the bottom of the cliff, Smith is on my heels, and the wind carries away whatever Sanderson is saying to de Vere while he holds on to the line tethered to de Vere's boat.

"What the fuck are you doing here?" I ask as I pound down the pier toward him.

As soon as I get close, I slow as I take in de Vere's appearance. His face is busted up and bleeding. His shirt is covered in blood and dirt. But it's his eyes that are the most disturbing as soon as they lock on me. They're wild. Frenzied. Like I was right and he's lost his goddamned mind.

"If you're gonna fucking kill me, just do it. Don't send your people after me, you fucking coward. At least have the balls to do it yourself!"

"What the fuck are you talking about?" The boat bumps the rub rails as I approach.

De Vere jumps out of the boat and onto the dock. "First I have to dodge the Russians, and now your dreadlocked giant tries to fucking kill me. Rammed my car, shoved me over the cliff. I crawled out and up the rocks before he could finish me off. You're a lot of things, Forge, but I didn't take you for a pussy-ass bitch who lets other people do your dirty work for you."

The words coming out of de Vere's mouth don't make sense. Goliath is here. What de Vere is accusing him of is impossible.

"You're fucking crazy. Goliath wouldn't do that, even on my orders."

"Then how many other white, dreadlocked giants are there running around on this island who work for someone who wants me dead? Because I'm coming up with *nothing*."

I grab my phone and tap the screen until I pull up Goliath's number. "I'll call him right now. He's here, not in Ibiza."

"Bullshit. I know what I saw. You don't have to lie anymore, Forge. I quit. I'm done. I didn't even fucking kill Isaac Marco."

My phone slides from my nerveless fingers at de Vere's bomb of a confession.

"What . . . what did you say?" My voice comes out hoarse as my mind races and blood roars in my ears.

Blood wells from a cut on de Vere's face and rolls down his cheek. "I didn't kill him. It was a fucking accident. Sure, I shouldn't have let an eleven-year-old drive my fucking boat, but I thought his brother was watching him. He was just a kid. I was passed out. It was a *fucking accident.*"

An eleven-year-old kid. No. No, that can't be true.

"What the fuck are you talking about?"

De Vere's busted lip curls. "My employee's little brother. He was the one at the helm that day. It's still fucking my fault, because I didn't know Littleton was passed out too. That's why I took the blame. I wasn't about to let an eleven-year-old's life be ruined because of something I was too stupid to prevent."

The rage I've been holding on to for years twists into a sea of confusion.

"A kid?"

De Vere jams a bloody hand into his hair, turning it a rusty red. "I couldn't let the truth get out. I had the protection of money and my title, but the Littletons only had the protection I could give them."

Blood roars in my ears when I think of everything I've done for the last ten fucking years . . . because I thought de Vere . . . "Jesus fucking Christ."

"It's the truth, Forge. I'm sorry. I'm so fucking sorry." His voice cracks, and his anguished expression makes me believe he's sincere.

"Why the fuck didn't you tell me?"

"You were out for blood. I let you take mine."

"Fuck. Fuck!" I tilt my head back and yell. "What a fucking mess."

That's when I hear a gunshot. De Vere opens his mouth to say something, but his body jerks and he stumbles backward.

"De Vere?" I take a step toward him, but he tumbles off the pier and into the water just as there's another shot.

Sanderson gasps as I lunge for him. Before I can reach him, blood blooms on his shirt, and another round hits Smith in the head.

I don't think. I throw myself off the dock.

Bullets hit the water, but I hold my breath. De Vere is sinking beneath the surface, and I grab his arm and pull him beside me. Blood, whether from the gunshot wound or his accident, floats on the current.

More shots hit the water as I swim us under the pier and up toward the shore where we'll be covered, but my mind isn't on de Vere, even if it should be. All I can think about is Indy.

I have to get to her. I have no fucking clue who is shooting at us, but it doesn't matter. *I have to get to her.*

I break the surface beneath the concrete pillars of the pier and haul de Vere's lifeless body onto the rocks beside me. He's unconscious. Maybe dead.

But Indy might still be alive. No. She *has to be alive.* I can't fucking lose her now. *I won't.*

Adrenaline dumps into my system, and the world goes silent as I try to figure out what the fuck is going on.

De Vere said Goliath hit him and ran his car off a cliff. Why? It doesn't make sense. Goliath would never do something like that . . . unless there's something I'm missing.

Could we have been double-crossed by Federov? Would he kill me to keep me away from Indy?

Without knowing a motive, I have no fucking clue what I'm walking into, but it doesn't matter.

I'll walk into a hail of bullets if it means saving Indy.

*O*h my God. Oh my God.

"Goliath?" My voice shakes as I say his name, and the man who I clung to for support in Prague steps out from behind a tree and turns his rifle on me. But there's already a gun pointed at my head.

Oh my God. Oh my God. This isn't happening. This can't be happening. Did Goliath just kill Jericho?

"What the fuck is going on?" My father, who jumped in front of me as soon as the first gunshot sounded, barks out. His blue eyes are razor sharp as they swing from Kostya's body to Goliath, and finally to Dorsey, who murdered Kostya in cold blood, before turning the gun on me and my father.

"Give me the gun, old man. I know you've got one."

"Dorsey?" I croak her name, and she barely spares a glance at me.

"Shut up, you whiny bitch. I've had enough of your mouth."

In her navy polo, she steps toward us and holds out her hand as Goliath comes closer, his rifle cradled in his arms. "Gun, or I shoot you in the fucking head right now."

My father yanks up his pant leg, exposing his holster. Dorsey rips the pistol from the leather and steps back as Goliath closes the distance.

"You got them all?" Dorsey asks.

"Forge dove off the pier. I don't know if I hit him. De Vere, Sanderson, Smith, and Federov's other guy at the chopper are all dead."

My stomach revolts and my heart lurches. *Jericho could still be alive. Oh God, please let him be alive. I can't lose him. Not now. Please.*

"This wouldn't have been necessary if you'd done your job and killed de Vere. How could you screw that up? You knew the plan. Now we have to make this look like a murder-suicide situation with way too many fucking players. Goddammit," Dorsey says to Goliath as she grips a pistol in each hand.

"Baby, I'm sorry. I didn't think there was any way he could survive that cliff. He's a tough motherfucker to kill."

Baby?

My gaze cuts between Dorsey and Goliath, and

confusion muddles my thoughts. "What the hell is going on?"

My pulse pounds in my ears as Dorsey's cruel smile sends chills across my skin. *She's crazy.* "After the six longest months of my fucking life being at Forge's beck and call, we're finally cleaning up all the loose ends before we live happily ever after . . . with *my father's money.*"

"Who was your father?"

"Sit down and shut up." Dorsey waves one gun at the metal table where Forge first handed me a check for a million dollars, then turns to Goliath. "Go find Forge's body. If he's not dead, I want to kill him myself."

Goliath walks to her side, presses a kiss to her lips, and jogs to the cliff stairs as I stare at Dorsey with my mouth gaping open.

"You fucking whore bitch. How dare you?" My father roars in anger and lunges toward her.

"We don't need you for this, Federov."

She pulls the trigger twice, and my ears ring with the percussion. My father stumbles back, almost knocking me over as he grips his chest. His head smacks the concrete with a sickening thud.

"No!" I drop to my knees, but Dorsey shoves the barrel of the gun in my face.

"Go sit the fuck down unless you want to die right now. Because I hate to break it to you, but this story doesn't have a happy ending for you either."

"Why? How?"

"Well, it all started twenty-five years ago when Isaac Marco fucked my mother and walked away without looking back . . ."

*R*ock shreds my clothes as I swim around the island to the rear stairs, the only other way to get up to Isla del Cielo. Isaac didn't just choose this island because it was beautiful, but also because it was nearly impenetrable. Sure enough, one of my tenders is anchored off the back side of the island.

De Vere was probably telling the truth. Goliath could have left, tried to kill him, and then came back to take the rest of us out.

But why?

That doesn't matter. The only thing that matters is getting to Indy and keeping her alive.

The back stairs are wooden, and alarmed, but I step over the sensors, just like Goliath would have.

I can't fucking believe this is happening.

I reach the top of them, wishing I had a fucking

weapon, but I sure as hell don't. I duck behind the chopper and spot blood pooling on the ground.

Fuck.

One of Federov's security guards has a knife through his throat. *Jesus Christ.* He didn't even have a chance to go for his gun—which is still in his shoulder holster.

I grab it and check the chamber. Locked and loaded.

Sticking close to the walls of the buildings, I move closer to the house. I pause when I hear Dorsey's voice.

What the fuck is going on here? I slip inside silently and peek over the counters.

Dorsey has a gun to Indy's head. Betrayal and terror grip my fucking soul with their bone-chilling fingers. I raise the pistol but have no shot. I can't take the chance of hitting Indy.

Ducking down, I move through the kitchen, but I can't pull the trigger. Not if there's a chance I could hit her. With no good options, I grab a glass off the counter and toss it through the open glass doors, trying for a distraction.

As soon as it shatters, Dorsey moves and I charge forward, squeezing the trigger.

But she drops to the ground, and I fucking *miss.*

Indy's shocked gaze cuts to me, and Dorsey pops up with a gun in either hand. One points at Indy and the other is zeroed in on my chest.

"Fuck you, Forge. Hands up, throw the gun down.

Get the fuck out here before I shoot her in the goddamned head in front of you. Do you want to see her brains splatter all over the table? Because that's exactly what's going to happen."

"Why the fuck are you doing this?"

Dorsey's normally placid face is smug as fuck as she moves behind Indy. "I was just about to get to the good part of the story. I'll let you hear the end before I end you. After all, I've waited so fucking long to tell you. And now you'll know why you and your little bitch are going to die."

I walk toward the door, gun still in hand, but I have no shot. "Let her go. Whatever you want, you can have it. Take it and go. Leave Indy alone."

Dorsey's head tilts to the side, and I catch a glimpse of a grin that's nothing short of evil.

How the fuck did this happen?

"You don't make the rules anymore, Forge. I'm calling the shots. Toss the gun on the ground and sit the fuck down if you don't want a bullet in her head before story time is over. Because that's exactly what's going to happen as soon as Goliath gets back."

Goliath. It was because of his trusted and glowing recommendation that I hired Dorsey earlier this year . . . which means whatever their plan was, it started long before today.

With no choice but to obey, I squat down and lower the gun to the ground.

"Isaac was her father, Jericho," Indy says.

Dorsey reaches out and smacks her in the head with the butt of the gun. "Shut the fuck up. It's my story."

Blood blooms at Indy's temple, and her knees give way. With Dorsey's attention split, I charge at her, but she pops off a round that misses Indy's crumpled form by an inch.

"No more sudden movements, Forge. Kick the gun to me."

I thought nothing could be worse than knowing I couldn't save Isaac from that wreck, but I was wrong.

As I kick my only weapon toward Dorsey, while she holds a gun on the woman I love, I know what true torture is. But the clawing fear in my gut isn't going to save us. I have to *think*.

"Isaac didn't have any children, Dorsey. It's fucking impossible. I don't know who lied to you."

The gun in her left hand jabs in my direction. "He sure as fuck did. He just didn't know it. He stopped to see my mom every time he was in Norfolk. At least, until the time he knocked her up and never came back. She would never tell me who my father was. Not until she was *dying* last year. Then she told me everything."

Norfolk, Virginia. It was a port Isaac frequented. I can't deny that.

"Then if Isaac was your father, you know he wouldn't want this."

She glares at me, her expression contorted with rage.

"I don't give a fuck what he would've wanted. I wanted a *father.* Little bitch over here had one scouring the world for her, and mine didn't even know I existed before de Vere killed him."

"De Vere didn't kill Isaac, Dorsey. It was an accident. That's what he came here to tell me. It was an eleven-year-old at the helm that day. De Vere took the rap for it because he didn't want to ruin the kid's life."

A mix of emotions play across Dorsey's face, and her mouth moves silently. "That's . . . that's not true. De Vere must have lied. He had to die. I've been waiting for a goddamn year for you to take our revenge. But you didn't have the balls to fucking end him. That's when I decided to do it myself. And then this bitch came along, and you forgot about avenging Isaac. *You did this to yourself.*"

"What the fuck do you want, Dorsey? De Vere's dead. Isaac's gone. You want money? Because you can have it all. Every single goddamned penny, but you have to let Indy go first."

"Shut the fuck up! Don't tell me what to do."

Indy's terrified gaze locks on me, and I can read her lips. *"I love you no matter what."*

Resolve hardens in me like steel. I will not lose her. Not now. Not ever.

"There's at least ten million in the safe, bills, gold, and diamonds. Take it and go. I won't report it. I won't even look for you."

"Like I won't take it all anyway? Fucking idiot. And you're damn right you won't look for me, because you'll be *dead*, and Goliath and I will be gone."

Her finger curls around the trigger, and I dive toward Indy. Gunshots ring out, coming from beyond the cliff, and I wait for Dorsey to fire. When she doesn't, I look up to see a cruel smile twisting her lips.

"Goliath just killed whoever was still breathing. Thanks for hiring such competent people, Forge. And thanks for working him so hard he couldn't have a personal life and was as desperate for a human connection as you. It was so easy to turn Goliath against you. And to blame everything he did on Koba. That poor bastard really deserved a medal for being loyal, even though you doubted him." She laughs, and the barrel of the gun bobs.

"Everything else was too easy to pin on de Vere, especially the kidnapping in Prague. All I had to do was hire guys from Bratva that sold him drugs, and you never thought to dig further into who paid them. Although, if my guy had been able to kidnap your bitch wife in Mallorca and ransom her back to you, we never would've had to bother with you in Prague. But, of course, you had to have a backup plan to get her home after the chopper was fucked."

Jesus fucking Christ.

How did I miss it? I never once suspected Goliath.

After I saved his life fifteen years ago, I never thought he'd betray me.

"Isaac wouldn't want this, Dorsey," I tell her, saying anything I can to buy time to come up with a way to take her out and save Indy.

"I wouldn't know what Isaac would want, because *you* got him, and I didn't even know he was my father until he was already dead! How is that fair? You got everything that should've been mine! Now I'm taking it back." She lowers the barrel of one gun to Indy's head.

"No!"

I launch myself at Dorsey's feet, and she stumbles back as she fires both pistols. The bullets strike the cement, sending fragments flying, before another shot rings out.

But it doesn't come from Dorsey. Bastien de Vere charges across the pool deck and fires again and again, pumping rounds into Dorsey's body.

She hits the cement and both pistols fall from her fingers. Blood bubbles out of her mouth.

I grab a gun and turn to de Vere, but he's only focused on Dorsey. "Go join your fucking boyfriend who tried to kill me. I hope you both enjoy hell."

She gurgles, and her head slumps to the side.

De Vere looks at me and the weapon I have trained on him. "If you want to shoot me, go right a-fucking-head. I'm tapped out." He tosses the rifle he must have taken from Goliath on the table, slumps into a chair, and tears the bottom of his shirt off to press against the wound in his chest.

Indy scrambles over to her father, leaning over him. "No! No!"

I'm on my knees beside her in a second, sidestepping around the pool of blood spreading out from beneath Dorsey.

But there's no blood under Federov's torso, only where his head hit the ground. *Internal bleeding from the gunshot wound?*

Indy shakes him, pressing her forehead against his chest, until the Russian coughs and blinks his eyes.

"Oh my God. Oh my God. You're alive." Indy's whispers come out on the edge of a sob.

"The vest," he chokes out.

I look down at his chest, where the burn marks are on his shirt and suit jacket. "You're wearing Kevlar. Fuck." A sigh of relief leaves me as I hold out a hand.

"Damn right. Never go anywhere without it. Can't be too careful."

Indy's tears fall as we help the old man up. The bullet fragments fall from his chest, and I rip my shirt off to press against the blood spilling from his skull.

"Not a bad idea, Russian," de Vere says. "Because this hurts like a bitch without one."

A private medevac left first with de Vere, the bullet still lodged in his chest and his skin an unhealthy gray. Before, I wouldn't have cared if he lived or died, but now knowing the truth about Isaac's death, I hope he pulls through.

My contacts with Interpol are on their way to assist the local police who arrived shortly after the medevac, along with a host of attorneys to ensure there are no issues. In the meantime, we've provided all the information we gleaned from Dorsey and Goliath. We're all still reeling from the shock, especially me.

How the fuck didn't I realize what was happening? As the coroner and his assistants load bodies onto boats, I know I'll never forgive myself for the loss of so many lives under my watch.

I make it clear to the authorities that Goliath and

Dorsey's deaths were self-defense, and the police agree to take de Vere's statement at the hospital when he recovers from the surgery he'll undergo as soon as they land.

Once Interpol and the attorneys arrive, the process of explaining what happened begins all over again. They stay until the early hours of the next morning, until Indy, Federov, and I are all fading from fatigue, but all parties involved agree on one very important item. What happened on Isla del Cielo will not receive media attention, and the investigation will be conducted confidentially. Federov has gone so far as to threaten to buy and shut down any media outlet that even thinks about publishing the story.

After everyone is finally gone, I press a kiss to the top of Indy's head. "Go to bed, Ace. You're beat."

She looks at me and her father, who will be staying in one of the guest rooms tonight.

"I think it's time for all of us to go to bed. Although, I don't know if I'll be able to sleep. I don't even know what to think. Or to say," she says with a shake of her head. "Dorsey . . . was . . ."

"Wrong," I tell her.

"What do you mean, wrong?" Indy and her father look at me with confusion.

"Isaac had an injury when he was a kid. He couldn't have children. He went through all the testing. He may have visited Dorsey's mother when he was in port . . . but he wasn't Dorsey's father."

"Jesus Christ." Federov leans on the kitchen counter. "I would tell you to check your employees' backgrounds better, but I am guilty of trusting those I shouldn't have either. I thought I took care of all the threats to India's life when I removed my second in command. He was responsible for Summer's kidnapping. For the ransom. For all of it."

It's one more shock in a long day packed with them. "*Your* second in command took Summer?" Indy asks.

He nods. "I am thankful she was not hurt, but I cannot find it in myself to regret that she was taken because it led me to you." Federov covers Indy's hand with his. "I promise I will make it up to you both. She will be treated as my daughter as well. Like you have said to me, family is more than blood."

A soft smile crosses Indy's face, and she places her other hand on top of his and squeezes. "That . . . that would mean the world to me. And to her."

The older man's entire face softens when he looks at her.

Regardless of how this life-changing chain of events came about, I think all three of us are so fucking grateful to be standing here right now. I can't bring back the lives that were lost, but I will honor my people and make sure their families are provided for.

I step behind Indy and lower my palms to her shoulders. "You need sleep."

"I know, but I still can't believe they were behind the kidnapping in Prague," Indy says with disbelief underlying every word. "I never thought . . . since Goliath got shot too . . ."

"Best way to throw off suspicion is to get injured," I reply, "but I didn't see it either. Not after fifteen years of unquestionable loyalty."

"Women are persuasive creatures," Federov adds, his gaze tracking from Indy's face to mine. "I am glad my daughter persuaded me to see the error of my judgment regarding you, Forge. I should not have interfered. I will not interfere again. You have my word and my blessing."

"Thank you, sir," I say, and I mean it.

"One question more, though. What does this mean for your grudge with de Vere?" Federov asks.

"I think it's safe to say that's over," I reply, curling my arm around Indy. "I will never be able to repay him for what he did, even if I still want to strangle him for the stunt with the drugs."

Indy drops her head onto my shoulder. "Bastien will always be Bastien, but I think it's time for all of us to move on."

"We will drink to that before we sleep," Federov says as he rises. "Where is your vodka? We need a toast to burying old hurts, celebrating life, and most of all, to your marriage."

Indy spins around in the circle of my arms. "Are we still married?"

"I have no idea. I haven't been able to get in touch with the judge. He works on island time. Either way, it doesn't matter to me." I lift her left hand to my lips and press a kiss to the back, next to her ring. "If we're divorced, I'm going to do it all right the second time."

EPILOGUE

India

Five months later

I'M GETTING MARRIED. *Again.* Except this time, things are wildly different. The perfume of fresh flowers scents the air of Isla del Cielo, wafting through the master bedroom where Summer puts the finishing touches on the gown she designed for me. It's going to be the centerpiece of her new bridal couture collection.

As thrilled as she was to discover her talent for creating wedding dresses, Summer still might want to strangle me, because she's had to adjust it three times in the last three weeks. My belly keeps surprising us both.

I'm pregnant. *With twins.* One boy and one girl. I shouldn't even be surprised, because we're talking about the Kraken and its wildly effective virility.

I'll never forget the look of awe on Jericho's face when we first heard the heartbeats, and then later saw the ultrasound. He reached out, tracing their outlines on the screen, and turned to me with tears in his eyes.

Irina and Isaac will never have to wonder if they're loved. They won't have to wait years to find a family or make their own. They will know every second of every day how grateful we are to be blessed with them.

Surprisingly, at least to me, Summer handled the news about Nina and Federov incredibly well. When he arrived on the island yesterday, she greeted him with a giant hug and a kiss on the cheek. She calls him Pops, which he absolutely adores.

His prognosis hasn't improved, but so far, he's defying the doctor's odds of survival. Part of me thinks that he's just too stubborn to miss the chance to walk me down the aisle. I'm praying he's just as stubborn when it comes to hanging on to hold his grandbabies in his arms after they're born. I'm betting on him. I don't even want to think about the alternative.

"I still think you should've waited until after the babies were born to have the wedding. As incredible as this dress looks now, the lines would have been even better without the wonder twins."

I almost drop the ring box as I start laughing. "You

think Jericho would've let that happen? I had to negoti-ate, while naked, to get him to even wait this long so you could *make* the dress. I think his exact words were something along the lines of—'you're mine, the babies are mine, and I want my wife back as soon as fucking possible.'"

"Ewww. You could've left out the naked part from that story. Also, stop laughing. I don't want to stab you."

"*Ewww* from you? Really?"

"He's my ex-brother-in-law who's soon to be my brother-in-law again. Don't make it awkward. I already had to hear about the Kraken, and I'll never be able to forget it."

It's impossible for me to obey her no-laughing order this time.

"Y'all about ready? Because I've never seen a more impatient groom waiting to see his bride."

Holly's Southern twang comes from the doorway, where she's wearing another of Summer's creations. The pale aquamarine dress looks *incredible* with her curvaceous figure and dark hair.

Summer might have spent more time on her dress and Holly's than mine, because she was determined to make them the most sought-after dresses of the year. With the number of inquiries she's already getting based on Holly's social media posts, I think my little sister is well on her way to establishing her new brand in a big, splashy fashion. I haven't told her yet that I want her to design all my dresses for my poker games after the babies are born.

"I'm ready as soon as Summer quits fussing over my dress."

My sister grunts as Holly steps aside to allow Alanna to slip into the room. "Jericho sent me—"

Another round of laughter fills the room as Summer finally stands and nabs the ring box from my hands. "Fine. Fine. He can have you as you are. No returns this time."

Alanna lifts her hand to her mouth as her eyes glisten. "Oh, Indy. You look beautiful." She swallows and holds out a hand. "I've never been so glad to have a daughter divorced so I could see her get remarried."

I walk toward her, and she grips my fingers tightly. "Thank you," I whisper.

We both blink back the tears as she leads me toward the sliding glass door that opens to the pool and patio, where the wedding guests are waiting. Holly hands Summer her flowers, and they head out the door. Instead of a traditional bridal party processional, Summer will be standing near the cliffs, opposite the groomsmen, and Holly will join her once she finishes singing.

"I'll give you two minutes, and then I'm starting," Holly says with a smile, and I'm grateful to call her a friend.

Creighton Karas and Lincoln Riscoff, who forgave Jericho and my father for the rocky business negotiations, are standing up for Jericho today. Riscoff insisted Karas pay back the winnings on the bet they made over six months ago, because they were *both* right about when Jericho would say "I do"—within six months and a year.

My father meets Alanna and me at the doorway. "It is my honor to share the privilege of walking our daughter down the aisle together," he says to Alanna. The two have become friends since he moved to Ibiza, against doctor's orders, to be close to Summer and me.

They each hold out an arm to me. "Are you ready, sweetheart?" Alanna asks.

"Absolutely." My flowing dress flutters in the ocean breeze as I lay one hand on top of each of theirs.

The first notes of the piano sound, and we step outside as Holly sings the most incredible cover of Ruelle's "I Get to Love You."

Jericho's stormy gray eyes shimmer like moonlight on the ocean as soon as he catches sight of me. Pure, radiant happiness beams from him as he watches me come toward him. The guests seem to fade away as I near him, until all that's left is us.

My mother and father press kisses to my cheeks, and Jericho takes my hands and raises them to his lips.

As he brushes his lips across my hands, he says, "I would marry you over and over, every day for the rest of our lives. Once, twice, a thousand times. I don't care. You're mine until the last breath leaves my body."

It takes everything I have to keep the happy tears from tipping over my lids. I didn't know it was possible to love someone this much.

"Until the last beat of my heart," I tell him.

He drops to one knee, cups his hands around my belly, and looks up at me as he whispers to my bump the way he's done dozens of times since we learned I was pregnant.

"I'm holding my world in my hands. This is true wealth beyond measure."

ACKNOWLEDGMENTS

To my dearest readers—you will never know how much you have changed my life, and for that, I owe you infinite thanks. I can only hope that I've had a tiny positive impact on your life as well. I know what it's like to need an escape. I know what it's like to desperately want to lose yourself in someone else's story to take your mind off your own reality. That is why I write. For YOU. For my dreamers and my runaways who need an escape from the world.

To my team—Jake, Jamie, Emily, Mo, Pam, Donna, Natasha, Kim, Julie, Anthony, Madelyn, and Ty—I am beyond blessed to work with such positive, incredible people who have helped me every step of the way. My books would not be what they are if not for you. I could write a chapter of thanks for each of you and it still wouldn't be enough. I'm so grateful to have found my tribe, and I can't wait to see what awe-inspiring things the future holds for all of us.

To everyone who spreads the word about my books—I SEE YOU, and I appreciate the hell out of you. You're a gift to this amazing book world. Thank you for all that you do.

ALSO BY MEGHAN MARCH

FORGE TRILOGY:

Deal with the Devil

Luck of the Devil

Heart of the Devil

SIN TRILOGY:

Richer Than Sin

Guilty as Sin

Reveling in Sin

MOUNT TRILOGY:

Ruthless King

Defiant Queen

Sinful Empire

SAVAGE TRILOGY:

Savage Prince

Iron Princess

Rogue Royalty

BENEATH SERIES:

Beneath This Mask

Beneath This Ink

Beneath These Chains

Beneath These Scars

Beneath These Lies

Beneath These Shadows

Beneath The Truth

DIRTY BILLIONAIRE TRILOGY:

Dirty Billionaire

Dirty Pleasures

Dirty Together

DIRTY GIRL DUET:

Dirty Girl

Dirty Love

REAL DUET:

Real Good Man

Real Good Love

REAL DIRTY DUET:

Real Dirty

Real Sexy

FLASH BANG SERIES:

Flash Bang

Hard Charger

STANDALONES:

Take Me Back

Bad Judgment

ABOUT THE AUTHOR

Making the jump from corporate lawyer to romance author was a leap of faith that *New York Times*, #1 *Wall Street Journal*, and *USA Today* bestselling author Meghan March will never regret. With over thirty titles published, she has sold millions of books in nearly a dozen languages to fellow romance-lovers around the world. A nomad at heart, she can currently be found in the woods of the Pacific Northwest, living her happily ever after with her real-life alpha hero.

She'd love to hear from you. Connect with her at:

Website:
www.meghanmarch.com
Facebook:
www.facebook.com/MeghanMarchAuthor
Twitter:
www.twitter.com/meghan_march
Instagram:
www.instagram.com/meghanmarch

CPSIA information can be obtained
at www.ICGtesting.com
Printed in the USA
LVHW032316260319
611967LV00002B/239